In a Mirror Darkly

Bob Stampfli

Order this book online at www.trafford.com
or email orders@trafford.com

Most Trafford titles are also available at major online book retailers.

This is a work of fiction. All of the characters, names, incidents,
organizations, and dialogue in this novel are either the products
of the author's imagination or are used fictitiously.

Printed in the United States of America.

ISBN: 978-1-4269-3971-6 (sc)
ISBN: 978-1-4269-3972-3 (e)

Trafford rev. 04/21/2011

North America & international
toll-free: 1 888 232 4444 (USA & Canada)
phone: 250 383 6864 • fax: 812 355 4082

"For now we see in a mirror darkly; but then face to face; now I know in part, but then shall I know even as also I am known."*

*I Corinthians 13:12, New Scofield Reference Bible, Oxford University Press, 1967 edition

Dedicated to Lucy Marie Stampfli

I.

As the Chevy droned through the moonlit evening, Ray Lennox, with his wife snuggled close to him reminisced about the past events which had brought him to this moment.

At eleven-thirty that evening, they had left the Lake City Airport to which Laura had driven the 15 miles from the farm. He had been discharged from the army that afternoon in Missouri and had flown immediately to Lake City. After spending two years in Germany, the young soldier's reunion with his wife was an exciting moment.

Ray had decided to join the army out of high school, since there was no future, so it seemed, on the Oak Hill farm, occupied now by his Grandfather Lennox. After his parents were killed a few years ago in an auto accident, he was left in sole possession of the farm. He and Laura Crane had been married 3 years ago, just before he went overseas, much to the consternation of her mother. Laura lived with her mother during the years that Ray was away, stationed in Germany.

Ray had served his first year in Missouri and received many passes to fly home to visit his young wife who was staying with her mother in Landville. Military life agreed with Ray. While going through basic training, he had done everything with such precision that he was kept in camp as an instructor. While home on furloughs, he had worn his uniform with such pride and dignity that a great many of his friends believed that the army had made him a little cocky. There were rumors that he intended to make a career of the army and that Laura would soon join him in Germany. The army they speculated would have much more to offer the young couple than the run-down old farm.

But it was natural for him to be returning home at this moment, returning to the farm which he owned. It was an ownership which he had acquired at a terrible expense—an ownership which he would have gladly given back.

As the car glided through the silver evening, Ray recalled that fateful summer afternoon three years ago when Gramp had come stumbling, without his cane, into the oak forest where Ray was examining the sizes of trees. The old man was slightly crippled, and Ray knew that something very bad had happened. Gramp told him that both of his parents had just been killed in a head-on crash at the bottom of Oak Hill. The parents were returning home from a shopping trip to Landville. As they proceeded up the hill and around a sharp curve, a drunk driver came barreling down the hill and failed to negotiate the turn. The cars met head on, sending both cars rolling into a ravine and down among the trees. After hearing the news, Ray sat petrified on a large rock scarcely hearing Gramp's consoling voice. Shortly after, he and the old man had gone down into Landville and made arrangements with the preacher and undertaker.

The shocking events had thrust Ray into a different world. Suddenly, he found himself with adult responsibilities, and he began to develop a new perspective on life. Shortly before the funeral, Gramp had told him about the 20,000 dollar life insurance premium that his parents had left him. He had heard them speak about life insurance, but at that time the words had little meaning. After the funeral expenses and farm bills were paid off, the amount had dwindled to about 12,000 dollars. The money was still in the Landville State Bank.

The young couple had been on the road for nearly an hour now and were only a few miles from home. Laura who had been sleeping stretched her arms toward the sun-visor, and Ray broke the silence.

"Well, honey, it's been a tiring day, but we're nearly there, just across a valley and up Oak Hill."

"Across the valley and up the hill," his wife repeated. "Oh, darling, it will be so nice finally to be home."

Oak Hill was synonymous with the farm. Part of the wooded farmland extended along the road they were traveling. The road formed the boundary between two townships and, thus, was called Townline Road. Tall, dark trees lined both sides of the road. Overhead, the moon seemed to glide through the branches. A warm breeze brushed their faces through the open car windows. Both were lost in thought.

Finally, Ray broke the silence, "With the money that's in the bank, and the 3,000 I've managed to save, I think we're off ta a good start. Besides, I think Gramp would also help us ta git started.

Laura smiled up at her husband.

"Yes, I know. I visited him some days when he was up at the farm. He has a nice big garden again, and he told me we can have whatever we want from the garden."

Grandpa Lennox owned a home in Landville but loved to spend time up on the farm. While Ray was away in the army, Gramp agreed to look after things. He was especially attracted to the forest and spent much time wandering around observing the changing features of nature.

Again, there was silence.

"You know what dearest?" Laura spoke cheerfully. "When you were away, I managed to save 2,500 dollars."

Ray looked surprised, "That's quite a bit for the little work you did!"

"Well, I believe Uncle Ed slipped in a little extra," Laura responded.

For over two years, Laura had worked at Uncle Ed's hardware store as a cashier. She loved the work and hoped to continue part-time, once she got settled on the farm.

Laura glanced out into the soft fall evening. Fireflies were popping in the bushes along the road. They were now going up Oak Hill, and Laura spoke solemnly, "You know Uncle John has always taken a liking to me. He bought me clothes and things that I needed. It wasn't much, just a few items. I thought I'd better accept them or I'd hurt his feelings."

Ray was silent for a moment. When he spoke his voice was glum. "Ya know how I was hopin' we'd never be indebted to your mother's family. She has never taken much of a likin' to me or my family. We will have to pay your uncle back. I'll offer him somethin' next time I see 'im."

"You owe Unk nothing," Laura spoke indignantly. "He will feel offended if you offer him any money. With his big trucking business, he'll never miss the little money he gave me."

Laura realized that Ray was still unhappy. Actually, he had a right to feel this way, since her family had had difficulty in accepting Ray as an in-law. All of Laura's relatives lived in Landville were successful in business.

Her father had run the town's only hardware store until he suddenly died of a heart attack at the age of fifty-two. Uncle John operated a prosperous trucking firm, and her Uncle Ed now operated the family hardware store. All of the town's merchants considered themselves of better class than the area farmers. When the relatives of Laura Crane discovered that she planned to marry the son of the poorest farmer in the area, they immediately voiced their opposition to the marriage. There were better, wealthier young men around who would be much more suitable.

Laura's mother, Mrs. Helga Crane, was the most remonstrative of all in her condemnation. Helga had been resentful, if not bitter, about the burgeoning relationship between her daughter and the farm boy. A young reporter employed at the *Landville Gazette* had also displayed keen interest in Laura. Everett Ernst was a dashing young man who was bound to go places in life. With strong urging from her family, Laura focused her attention on Ernst, but found him not her type. In the end she realized that Ray was her one and only love. "A farmer's wife!" Her mother had used the expression in derision. Laura argued that she loved country life and that she loved Ray, and nothing would ever separate them. With Ray, who was born and raised in the country, she would have a beautiful life.

Helga Crane had taken an intense dislike to Ray the moment the engagement was announced. Ray was a strong young man who had starred in both football and basketball at Landville High. He was the town's hero his senior year when he intercepted a pass and ran 70 yards for a touchdown. The heroic deed had won the league championship for the school. He was the talk of the town for weeks after. Some even suggested that he run for mayor. Helga, however, believed that the son of a farmer was receiving too much attention and that he was acting far too superior for his position.

Ray's friendship began with Laura had begun in his senior year when she was a junior. Laura was a beautiful and popular cheerleader, and after the young man's heroics on the football field drew community attention, she was attracted to him. He began to walk her home from school whenever he was off practice. Soon they were dating regularly. Amid intense gossip and criticism from the Crane family, Laura continued to see Ray. Laura, the family believed, must attend the local state university. With Ray, her life would be ruined.

While Ray was away in the army, attempts were made by the Crane family to disrupt or even sever the relationship. Mr. Everett Ernst was invited to Helga Crane's house on several occasions in the hopes that a friendship would develop between Laura and Everett. However, Laura did not care for the stiff formalism of the man. He spoke only about himself, concerning his accomplishments as a reporter. He invited Laura to travel with him to the "big city" for a weekend of fun, but she promptly refused.

Many other eligible young men were paraded before the young lady. Most were well-educated professionals who worked in area cities. But Laura was well aware of her mother's shenanigans. Amid the spreading gossip, Laura wrote a long letter to Ray describing all her mother's schemes and pledging her eternal love for him. During his next furlough, Ray stopped at the Landville State Bank and withdrew a large sum of money. Then he went to Lake City and bought a beautiful wedding ring for Laura. A few days later, after gathering the required documents and driving to the courthouse in an adjacent county, they were married by the justice of the peace. The Reverend Bruce Mattock from the Landville Community Church had refused to marry them. The Crane family was very influential in the church and had spoken negatively about a marriage, even though both Ray and Laura were lifetime members of the church. Now, Helga Crane would be scrutinizing the marriage and waiting to pronounce it a failure.

As the car crept up the hill along the final mile home, Laura thought about the new life which awaited them. They would do well on the farm because Ray was young and ambitious. He had promised to make something of the farm, which was now his farm, even though the place had always been destitute. The Lennox family was always poor by the standards of most of the villagers. But now there would be a big change, the big change that Ray had promised. Laura was just as optimistic as her husband. Also she had the added incentive to prove mother wrong. They were young: she was barely 21 and he was 22. Moreover, they were deeply in love, and nothing would ever destroy their beautiful union. They were nearly home now, home to a new life.

All the car windows were down as the newlyweds reached the crest of the hill. They could hear the rustling of tree branches, buffeted by the evening breeze. Soon the road wound around a sharp turn under some huge oak trees. The trees on the right side of the road were part of the forest which covered most of Ray's farm. Ray admired the huge trees but now harbored thoughts in opposition to family tradition. The trees had great value. Who would care if he harvested a few of them? The chirping of crickets filled the evening, while off in the forest, whippoorwills throbbed plaintively. This was an evening of peace and harmony.

As they rounded the final part of the curve, dark, moving forms appeared suddenly in the distance. Ray slowed the car as they approached two large animals hogging the middle of the road.

"What the devil?" Ray was startled. "Some farmer's cows have gotten out, I bet. I wish they'd git off the road." Two yellow eyes were glaring before them now. "I'm too tired ta be dodgin' cows out here in the middle of the night," Ray exclaimed.

"It will probably get scared and run back into the woods," Laura consoled.

Cautious, Ray slowed to a crawl. He had no intentions of colliding with a large animal, especially so close to home. On the crest of the hill, the woods and the underbrush were the thickest. Huge oaks lined both side of the road forming an archway, and fireflies flashed in the heavy undergrowth along the road.

Suddenly, an animal leaped in front of the car and froze, as Ray brought the car to a lurching stop. A horse stood before them glaring at the car. Ray opened the door, stepped out and yelled at the horse which then retreated a few yards but still maintained its stance in the middle of the road. Suddenly, another horse appeared behind the car.

"Looks like they've got us blocked in," Laura observed.

"Well, I'll be damned if that ain't one of Gramp's old horses!" Ray concluded as he got in the car and honked the horn. "They're runnin' around loose in the woods at night."

"They're really frisky," Laura rejoined.

"Well, I'm not goin' ta let two old nags stop us when we're so close ta home." As he spoke, he opened the door and jumped out. Then he picked up gravel and threw some at both horses. "Shoo, git out ah here!" he shouted. Both animals retreated a few feet. Finally, he made some lunges at the beasts, and they promptly disappeared into the undergrowth. Ray stood for a few minutes glaring into the forest. Now even the whippoorwills stopped crooning. An eerie feeling came over the young man as he stared into the night. Perturbed, Ray returned to the car to continue the short drive home.

"Were those Gramp's horses?" Laura inquired.

"They are!" Ray protested, "I wonder why they're out chasing around this time of night."

"They seem to be wild," Laura added.

"I know. I've never seen horses act so strange," Ray observed. "I wonder what he's been feeding those old nags."

"Well, they didn't seem old to me," Laura declared.

"They must be nearly 16 years old," Ray added as the car approached the crest of the hill. "I use ta play with 'em when I was a little boy. They liked me and followed me around like best friends."

""I guess Gramp told them that you were coming home tonight and they wanted to greet you," Laura chuckled as she spoke.

"If they're running wild who knows where they could be by morning," Ray asserted.

Soon they were at the farm driveway where massive oaks flanked each side. Drooping branches struck the top of the car. The house had several gables and in the moonlight looked stately and welcoming. They drove behind the house and parked their car next to Gramp's. Gramp had been at the farm for several days preparing for the young couple's homecoming.

They got out of the car and stood for a moment, listening to the sounds of the evening. Both were elated because they were home at last. They had been triumphant over the relentless condemnation of their relationship. Their deep love had been a shield, protecting them from hatred, ostracism, and lies. They had proven everyone wrong. They kissed as a warm breeze sang through the trees.

Ray broke the silence, "Oh, Laura, my sweet Laura, here we are home at last. Soon we'll have this farm put back together 'n' really surprise all those dummies down there." He pointed toward Landville as he spoke.

"I know that eventually we'll prove them all wrong," Laura consoled. "Wait until next year at this time and they'll all see how wrong they were." Laura spoke softly.

Then, hand in hand they walked around to the front of the house where they were greeted by the scent of blossoming phlox. They stood by the massive front door and thought about entering. Then Ray took his wife into his arms and kissed her tenderly. As a gentle wind whispered through the large trees, Laura's long, soft hair blew about striking them both in the face. Ray held her hair back, staring into her moonlit face.

"Forever and ever." Laura murmured.

Again they were locked in an embrace. Finally they returned to the car and retrieved two small suitcases. Then they entered the house through the unlocked backdoor leading to the kitchen. They entered and turned on the overhead light. Gramp had left a note on the table telling them to help themselves to fresh food in the refrigerator. Instead, they picked up their suitcases and headed for the downstairs master bedroom.

II.

THE BUILDINGS ON THE Lennox farm were located on the crest of the hill known as Oak Hill, because of the vast forest of oaks which covered the area.. The road continued eastward down the hill for another mile where it met the Land River. At this point it followed the river into Landville.

Since the farm consisted of 175 acres, it was a bit larger than the average farm in the area. Only about 80 acres of the farm was tillable. But the land consisted primarily of rocky loam, and the crop yield was usually rather poor. In fact, some years it was difficult to produce enough grain and hay to support a herd of 20 milk cows. The Lennox family had always lived in a state of semi-poverty, the poverty Ray Lennox hoped to defeat, and the poverty Helga Crane feared her daughter would inherit.

However, the farm also contained a forest of large, aged oak trees. The oaks were synonymous with the farm and covered the entire western slope all the way to the Land River. The oaks, stately and beautiful, were extremely valuable and were eyed by many sawmills in the area. Some of the mills had asked permission from Ray's father to harvest select trees. But the Lennoxes always desisted because the huge oaks represented the heart and soul of the farm. But Ray now had other ideas. The trees represented a source of instant cash, the cash he needed to provide an adequate life for Laura. In addition, he would be admired by the town's people as a young man who knew how to get ahead in the world. When Gramp heard about Ray's plans, the old man said that if any trees went he, too, would go.

An outstanding characteristic of the farm was the intense winds which rushed through the trees day and night, winter and summer. During the summer, even on the most pleasant days, the wind would rise toward evening. Also during the summer, storms would roar out of the west and maul the hill with heavy rain and hail. Often crops were left damaged. However, during the winter months, storms created major problems. At times the wind and snow could be relentless and horrendous, closing all the roads in deep banks of snow.

When the farm buildings were constructed at the turn of the century, accommodations had to be taken for the robust winds. Thus, the buildings on the Lennox farm were crafted to withstand the most extreme weather conditions. The two large buildings, the house and the barn, were built from oak taken from the huge forests which then spread across most of the township. Gramp who was then a small boy living in Landville observed the demise of the huge oak forests, as lumber was needed for construction of both villages and farms.

Smaller buildings on the Lennox farm did not fare as well against the harassing winds. In addition to the house and barn, there were two corncribs, one partially blown down; a large shed for machinery with a tree branch lying on its roof, and a chicken house with its roof blown off. Much work needed to be completed, in order to put the farm in a workable condition.

Although the barn was a fortress of oak, it was the house which was the pride of the community. The house had been listed in the County Historical Registry as an example of the sheer magnitude and opulence of a house built from oak. Laura had looked forward to becoming a part of this house — her new home where she would find love and happiness. Moreover, Ray had promised to make repairs on the house and also update all the other deteriorating buildings. He would return the farm to its original magnificence.

The front of the house was rectangular and had three gables facing Townline Road. The middle gable which provided entrance to the parlor consisted of a large double door crafted from oak. Both doors were hewed from 3 foot wide slabs of oak, provided by local trees. Adding to the solid features were well-defined grains, running the length of each door. The door on the right held a brass knocker which when sounded reverberated throughout the entire downstairs. This showpiece entrance was rarely used now since the backdoor provided easy access to the kitchen.

The two end gables also served practical uses. The gable on the left side created a dining room leading from the kitchen, and the one on the right formed an L-shaped parlor. This gable contained windows on all three sides providing views of the wooded hills surrounding the farm. Gramp loved to sit in the parlor during early evening to watch the various hues of red and orange as the sun sank beyond the western hills.

The celebrated house drew much attention. On weekends, especially, people from miles around drove down Townline Road to gawk at the house, an "amazing edifice of oak," a local newspaper had recently called it. Many people came expressly to take pictures when the lilacs and roses were in peak bloom. The joke going around Landville was that Laura should charge admission for guided tours of her house since this was the only way that money would ever be made from the farm.

Oak Hill was a delightful place in both summer and fall. There was an aura of tranquility created by the beauties of nature. In addition to the lofty trees, vast growths of lilacs and roses surrounded the house, creating pleasing fragrances. An abundance of daisies grew wild on the border between the front lawn and the woods. Various species of birds chirped and tweeted throughout the day, robins crooned plaintively at sunset. The Hill in the spring was a haven of peace, and beauty, the place that now was Ray and Laura's home.

III.

AT TEN A.M. RAY and Laura awoke in their huge master bedroom. After completing the morning toiletries, they set to work unpacking the suitcases and boxes of clothing which they had brought from Helga Crane's house in Landville. When they were about half done, the aroma of freshly brewed coffee invaded the room.

"Smells like Gramp's got some coffee all ready for us," Ray observed, sniffing the air appreciatively.

"Well, I hope he's got a nice breakfast waiting for us," Laura added.

The couple got dressed and walked down the short hallway leading to the kitchen. Here Grampa Lennox stood at the counter preparing pancakes and with a pot of brewing coffee sitting on the electric stove next to him. He turned and grabbed Ray's right hand and pumped it vigorously while with is other hand he grabbed Laura's wrist.

"Well, it's good old Gramp. How are ya? It's good ta see ya again! 'n' yer hard at work. That's what I really like ta see!" Ray exclaimed with a broad smile on his face.

"And it's nice ta see both of you again," Gramp obliged, "and this time yer here ta stay. Yer looking fit as a fiddle. The army must a taken good care of ya. I hear you even thought about stayin' in," Gramp proclaimed.

"Ya, but I thought it best ta git back here 'n' get something started on this old place." Ray affirmed.

"O.K., let's git started first with breakfast. Here Laura help me cook up some pancakes," Gramp ordered, pointing at the pancake mix resting on the counter. "This is your house now and you'll have ta take over."

Laura looked bewildered and then spoke leisurely, changing the subject, "Let's all go down to Wiesenhofs' tonight and celebrate our homecoming."

Wiesenhofs' was a fancy restaurant located on a bluff overlooking the Land River. Laura had eaten there many times with friends and relatives, but Ray had never been there. He was perturbed by the suggestion.

"We'll celebrate our homecoming right now with this breakfast. We have a lot a work ta do 'n' don't have time for fancy restaurants," Ray asserted.

Laura had made the statement frivolously and was surprised by Ray's reaction. Gramp came to her defense. "We'll have to take a little time ta talk about everything 'n' not get jumpy. Let's finish breakfast now 'n' then talk about what we'll do for the rest of the week." Gramp proclaimed.

Under Gramps tutelage, Laura made some pancakes and also fried bacon. As she worked she thought about all the days ahead and all the work that keeping her new home would require.

Ray was 18 when his parents were killed in the auto accident, and Gramp Lennox was the closest relative to whom he could turn for help and advice. His grandparents owned a house in Landville, where Gramp had spent most of his life working at a lumber yard. After the death of his wife, Gramp spent more and more time on the Hill, his name for the farm. After Ray enlisted in the army, the elderly man spent most of his time on the farm, preparing for Ray's return. Now, Ray would need much help from the knowledgeable old man.

To celebrate the special morning, Grandpa wore clean pair of overalls with cuffs rolled up to reveal the glossy black leather on the upper portion of the brogans. From an eye in the upper part of the bib, a gold watch chain dropped into a vertical slit in the bib. The watch had been handed down to him from his father who had brought it with him when he migrated from Wales. To top off his morning's dress, Gramp wore a light-blue dress shirt adorned with shiny, jeweled cufflinks. Gramp was in a jovial mood, after finally being all together on the Oak Hill farm.

Soon there was a large platter of pancakes and bacon resting on the kitchen counter. Then Gramp suggested that in order to honor the special day, they should eat at the large oak table in the dining room, instead of at the smaller kitchen table. Ray agreed to this idea, and they all grabbed plates and cups of food and drink and headed into the formal dining room.

"Well, how do ya like it in here, now, young lady? Ain't it beautiful," Gramp bragged.

"Oh, it's out of this world! This should be our regular place to eat!" As Laura spoke she marveled at the view and the stately layout of the room.

One of the gables formed the dining room and had windows on three sides. Spectacular views were offered of the forest and surrounding countryside. Laura was astonished at the multi-colored fall forest and the many flowers still in full blossom. Everywhere amid the towering trees were shrubs and flowers. There was a sea of yellow flowers growing in the woods where it joined the front lawn. Of special beauty, Laura noted a large bed of chrysanthemums which encircled the pine tree growing on the front lawn. The mums were various hues of red, orange and yellow. At this moment, the young wife thought about her friends and relatives in Landville. If only they were here now, certainly their attitude toward the farm would change. Perhaps later, after she had learned to cook a little better, she would have everyone up for dinner.

"I really love those mums you planted around the big pine," Laura spoke to Gramp as they continued eating breakfast. "They're so tall and sturdy."

"Well I planted 'em the year Ray left us. I s'pose they're nearly three years old now. they're getting' better every year."

"It was good of you, Gramp, ta come up here 'n' look after things when I was gone," Ray asserted. "We have a lot of work ta do, starting right after breakfast."

"Well, we should probably make a little plan first" Gramp suggested.

"Plan? I grew up here on the hill, 'n' the plan is ta git this old place goin' agin. The plan is ta show we kin live here without help from no one." Ray pointed in the direction of Landville as he spoke. "I'm the boss up here now, and there's the bosses' wife." Ray spoke teasingly now, smiling at Laura.

"Still we'd best git organized a little. We gotta do what works best up here on the hill," Gramp counseled.

Ray was lost in thought until Gramp made another suggestion. "Ya know you kin always rent out this here farm. It's been settin' fallow now for three years. The big operators 'round here know how ta handle this land 'n' make it produce somethin'."

Laura quickly added, "And then you could go to work for Uncle John. He'd love that."

"No, this farm is mine, 'n' I know how to run things around here! Like you said, we should have some good crops now 'n' come out ahead. We'll git goin' right away in the spring 'n' put our oats in," Ray assured.

There was silence and then Gramp spoke, "Ya don't have a tractor or equipment. What are we gonna do?"

After much discussion, Ray agreed to contact a neighboring farmer who had agreed to help Ray get started when he returned from the army.

With breakfast completed, Laura cleaned off the large oak table while Ray and Gramp discussed the problems immediately facing them. Ray became feisty when Gramp described the physical condition of the farm: wind-damaged buildings had to be repaired, rocks and stumps had to be cleared from a field where trees once stood, and many deteriorating fences needed to be replaced. The last item, Ray was well aware of, and he brought to Gramp's attention the fact that the two horses were running free.

"Ya know, Gramp, yer two old nags tried ta run us off the road last night at the big turn," Ray explained. "I thought I'd run into 'em 'n' had ta stop 'n' shoo 'em away. Are yer old horses loose in the woods?"

"Wail, I don't know fer sure. They were in the yard this mornin' when I got up. They're always rubbin' themselves on that old wood fence, 'n' I bet they pushed part of it over. That'll be another thing that needs fixin'," Gramp explained.

Ray was only 6 years old when Gramp delivered two colts to the farm one day in June. The boy immediately adopted them as if they were his own, and they became his playmates. He grew up with them, spending much time playing with them and grooming them. Now the animals were nearly 16 years old but still were quite frisky and had to be watched.

While Ray was away, Gramp took care of the horses, keeping them well fed and sheltered and treating them as his own. Now, however, the animals had more freedom than what they had as colts, for they roamed at will on and beyond the 175 acre farm. Since the fences had been badly neglected over the years, the two old horses had broken onto neighboring oat fields and cow pastures. Once, Gramp was sternly warned to control his horses or they would be shot.

After considering what Ray had just told him, Gramp spoke solemnly, "Wail, I giss I'll go out this afternoon 'n' git those two critters penned in. I was hopin' they could have a little freedom, but I giss that won't work."

"I'm surprised they didn't recognize me last night when I got out of the car," Ray asserted. "They seemed almost wild."

"You've been gone fer 3 years 'n' probably ya got an army smell," Gramp answered.

"Anyway, we'd better git those two old critters locked up so they don't go out 'n' do some serious damage. I think next week we'd better go out 'n' git all those fences fixed up," Ray conceded.

Before Gramp could answer, Laura entered the dining room from the kitchen where she had been taking inventory. "You know, I checked all the cupboards and there is not much food in the house. I thought that after church tomorrow we could go to the store and pick up a few things," she announced.

"I know mother always made a lot of bread 'n' rolls, 'n' we always had a big garden full of veggies. I don't want ta spend a lot of money buying things downtown when we got this here farm ta grow everything," Ray announced.

Listening to Ray, Laura grew concerned. Would she also have to start baking now? This was all outside her *modus operandi*. She could depend upon Gramp to help with some of the cooking and baking. But certain essential items would have to be purchased. Only poor people lived off the land, and they certainly were not poor.

Then Ray and Gramp spoke about plans to plant a garden in the spring. Gramp would plant his next to his house in Landville, and Ray would have his in the usual place behind the garage. Ray announced that they would buy seed at the grocery in the morning after church. Laura was unhappy with Ray's plans. She simply could not picture herself on hands and knees weeding a garden.

Sunday dawned as a beautiful fall day. Laura and Gramp prepared a simple breakfast. Gramp showed Laura how to cook oatmeal with the proper touch — not too think and not too thin. After a breakfast of oatmeal, coffee and toast, Gramp made a list of grocery items to be purchased at the grocery store in Landville. The store was open until 2:00 p.m. on Sundays.

As they were getting ready to leave for church, Laura invited Gramp to go with them. "There's going to be many of Ray's old friends visiting today since this is his first Sunday home. You really should meet them," Laura enjoined.

Gramp did not care for the church services in Landville. Usually, when he did attend, he fell asleep for most of the service. He felt more inspired by taking a walk through the forest on Sundays instead of going to church. And since this was a beautiful fall morning, he was headed for the woods.

"My friends are all out in the woods," he politely told Laura.

Even though Gramp had worked in the lumber business for many years, he always took a stand against the cutting of more and more oak timber. He had grown up in the area and loved the huge oak forests which covered the land. Often he would walk into the woods and disappear for most of the day. When asked where he had been, he would answer, "Oh, jist out coutin' trees."

Gramp was considered uneducated. He had not attended high school and would not say where he attended elementary school. Yet, Gramp loved books. In his bedroom on the farm there was a shelf filled with books. In the evening he would lie on his bed and read until he fell asleep. The small table next to his bed currently held two books, one titled *Walden* and the other, *The Grapes of Wrath.* Also lying about were several history books. Helga Crane never said much about the old man, except to pronounce him a little odd.

At 9:45, Ray and Laura parked their car in the lot behind the Landville Community Church, and the young couple, attired in Sunday finery, walked sprightly around to the front entrance. They were greeted on all sides by villagers on their way to church. Many of them noted in particular a change in Ray's physical features. His six-foot frame had matured considerably during the past 3 years. He was a muscular young man and walked ramrod straight. In general, his mien portrayed self-confidence and forcefulness. He wore the three-year old, dark brown suit which he had purchased for his high school graduation and which, now, he had somewhat outgrown. But clothed in his finery, Ray's composure was a bit overbearing. He hoped to show the congregants that he was at least their equal, if not even a little better than they. Laura admired her husband for the way he carried himself.

Laura wore a white dress trimmed in blue with a neckline that accentuated her well-developed breast. The black hair, which splashed around the top of her shoulders, had a blue ribbon pinned neatly on the right side. She was a small-framed girl who looked overpowered when walking next to her husband. She had friendly brown eyes that smiled at everyone.

Ray was surprised at the friendliness of everyone even as they took their seats in the back of the church. He did not see any of the Crane family and wondered if they were boycotting today's church services.

"I don't see yer mother anywhere," Ray observed.

"She sits down in front now. She'll be coming soon," Laura answered. Ray was surprised to hear this since the front of the church was reserved for outstanding citizens and the wealthy.

"You know mother gave a lot to the church after father died, so she feels that she should be up front with the Ernsts and some of her friends." Laura explained.

"Well, I hope she doesn't feel too good fer us in case we offer her a ride home," Ray declared.

"She and Addie Scrang always walk to and from church services. They've been doing it for years now," Laura recalled.

The Landville Community Church was located downtown on Main Street. It was a white frame structure built in the early part of the century. The highlight of the church was its huge double front door made from three-inch thick oak planks. Engraved on each door were crosses which covered the length and width of each. The doors were kept varnished and always looked shiny and new. Some members of the congregation once joked that the doors had to be heavy to keep the devil out. The church also had attractive stained glass windows donated by members through the years in memory of loved ones. A huge bell tower stood over the entrance of the church. It housed the bell which was always rung prior to the beginning of services. The tower was topped by a silver cross which the villagers admired because it reflected both the rays of the sun and the moon. The cross was especially admired in the evening when it captured the roseate hues of the setting sun.

The interior was typical of many smaller churches. A single aisle extended the entire length from the front entrance to the steps leading to what was called the sanctuary. On the right side of the sanctuary stood the pulpit, and on the left, stood the altar. Two huge leather-bound chairs completed the furnishings up front. One sat behind the pulpit against the wall, and the other behind the altar against the wall. A large stained-glass window highlighted the center wall at the front of the church. The extreme right front contained an organ where now the organist, J.S. Baker, was preparing sheet music in preparation for the morning service. Finally, he took his seat at the organ and waited for the church bell to ring.

Although the organist's full name was John Steven Baker, he preferred to be addressed simply as J.S. He was a meticulously dressed man of small physical stature who stood only five feet, six inches tall. He always wore dark clothes as if he were in mourning. He was a talented music teacher who made his living teaching piano lessons to village residents. Laura at one time had been his student.

J.S. had once been married to an attractive lady who owned a hair stylist shop in Lake City. They had lived together in a cottage on Main Street, and every morning each had gone their separate ways in pursuit of their careers. One evening his wife failed to return home. J.S. waited several days, and even then, the police could not locate her. He feared the worst but still waited for his beloved. Then one fall day many months later, he received the letter. His wife had run off with an airline pilot and now lived on the West Coast. She protested that she had grown tired of living with a stuffy little man in a stuffy little town. J.S. grieved for a long time as he accepted the condolences of the parishioners. Eventually, he acknowledged his fate and moved on with his life.

There was a hush as the congregants waited expectantly. Suddenly there was a commotion in the entryway of the church, and immediately Laura felt a little embarrassed. She knew who was arriving and simply stared straight ahead as her mother and Addie Scrang straggled in and marched confidently down the aisle to the front pew where they took their seats next to Everett Ernst.

Shortly the bell tower came alive with joyous pealing announcing the start of the Sunday service. In a moment, a thunderous chord emerged from the organ as J.S., rhythmically weaving to and fro, began to play a Bach chorale. Everyone was settled and now awaited the entrance of the pastor.

Then the Reverend Bruce Mattock, in his late forties and already balding, strode down the aisle, climbed the platform stairs and sat down in the large chair behind the pulpit. The Reverend, as usual on Sundays wore his preaching garb, a long black robe. He had been pastor at the Landville Community Church for over three years now and was well liked because of his sincerity and honesty. However most of the congregants felt sorry for him because of his abusive wife. Emma was a large, heavyset woman who was the ruler of their house.

Unfortunately, the pastor had developed a drinking problem and found comfort in the bottle. Alcohol bolstered his confidence and gave him courage to withstand his wife. One Saturday evening neighbors heard intense screaming and banging sounds, as if chairs were being thrown around, issuing from the house. The police arrived on the scene, put the pastor in handcuffs, and hauled him off to the local jail where he was allowed to sober up.

The next morning, Revered Mattock was in the pulpit as usual, from whence he apologized for his deviations. He claimed he had also apologized to his wife, and they had reached an agreement by which all domestic issues had been resolved. The congregation chuckled in amusement since similar resolutions had been made previously. Because his wife attended church only on the major holidays, the pastor felt free to express himself concerning domestic issues.

After the doxology and a hymn, the pastor delivered a short sermon on the topic of harmony in the marriage. Partners in marriage, he pointed out, are not truly partners unless they express their love for one another and also recognize the unique role each plays in a successful marriage. Reverend Mattock concluded his message by emphasizing: "A man's position is to rule over the woman, and holy scriptures will support me on this."

After the postlude Ray and Laura were nearly the first to leave the church. Ray grasped the waiting hand of the pastor who expressed his greetings, "It certainly is wonderful to have you back with us again. Laura told me that, perhaps, you would be arriving home this weekend."

"Thank you, Reverend Mattock. It's always swell ta come to church 'n' hear one of yer sermons." Ray tried complimenting.

"Well, thank you. We'll see you again next Sunday. I know you and Laura will be successful in your new lives together."

Both said goodbye, walked down the front steps, and waited for Helga Crane and Addie Scrang.

After more greetings and well wishes from old friends who expressed their delight in seeing Ray, Mrs. Addie Scrang followed by Mrs. Helga Crane appeared on the steps. Addie Scrang, who was over 70, was a notorious town gossip. She approached Ray inquisitively, head cocked a little to one side.

"Well, yer back. How's everyone treatin' ya? Yer lookin' good too, Laura. We was late fer church today because my front door got stuck, 'n' I couldn't get it open. Yer Ma finally come and give it a big kick, 'n' it went right open, giss I'll have one of the boys —"

"How are ya, Ray?" Helga cut her friend off. "I see ya made it back safe 'n' sound." As she spoke she looked her son-in-law over carefully.

Before Ray could answer, Helga Crane gave an order: "I want both of you over for lunch now. I've got some really good sandwiches all made up."

"But mother," Laura protested, "We have to stop for some groceries. We have practically nothing to eat up at the house."

"That store is open 'til two. There's plenty of time," Helga asserted.

Just then, Everett Ernst walked by on the way to his car. He gave a perfunctory wave to everyone.

After a momentary silence, Laura made a proposal, "By the time you two walk home and get lunch ready, we can easily buy our groceries and get back to your house."

Helga thought about the proposal for a moment and then conceded, since the grocery store was only four blocks away.

IV.

Since her father had died suddenly of a heart attack when she was just 13 years old, Laura grew into maturity living alone with her mother. The mother attempted to dominate every phase of the daughter's life, even after she had matured into an active young lady. Then Laura attempted to break away from her mother's dominance by taking weekend hiking trips or by spending several days with her many friends who lived in the area. On several occasions when Gramp had some work to do up on the hill, Laura rode along simply to investigate the livability of the huge house. In the near future the house would be her dwelling place. Helga was always perturbed whenever her daughter made the trip up to the farm.

Laura was an attractive, vivacious, and athletic young lady who had spent three years as a high school cheerleader. During her senior year, Uncle Ed gave her a pair of skis on her seventeenth birthday. Soon she and her friends were skiing down the hills around Landville. She looked forward to introducing the sport to Ray.

Most of the villagers expressed their concern about seeing the popular young woman moving up to the hilltop farm. They insisted that she was not suited for such a life and would soon realize her mistake. Moreover, Ray was not a farmer, and he could not depend upon the old man who lived contentedly in the village. Gramp had even spoken to some of the villagers about the risks of trying to make a living up on the hill. Now pressure was being placed upon Laura to persuade her future husband to sell the farm and find a job in the village. Laura realized that this idea would not work, because she knew about Ray's determination to make it good on the hill, even though his parents had experienced nothing but despair and futility there.

Helga Crane lived in a small frame house in Landville near the state highway that led south to Lake City. Laura was born and raised in this house which consisted of four rooms downstairs and a partially built upstairs with just one bedroom. All the windows in front had green shutters, which gave the house a colonial look. A large hill sloped toward the back yard of the house. During her younger days Laura and her friends would climb the hill and play in the woods which crowned its top. In the winter, village officials would close the street beneath the hill and both children and adults would sled down it, coasting nearly a half mile onto the frozen Land River. Mrs. Crane was reluctant to see her daughter go sledding for she always feared for her daughter's safety.

From the top of this same hill one could look far down the valley to the southeast; and to the west, one could see Oak Hill and the gabled roof of the Lennox house. On another hill on the northern fringes of the valley and overlooking the Land River was the Landville Memorial Cemetery where dead of all faiths were laid to rest. It was in this cemetery that the ancestors of both Laura and Ray reposed.

Ray was apprehensive as he pulled the Chevy up in front of his mother-in-law's house. He knew that he would have to prove to his in-laws for once and for all that, through drive and dedication, a good living could be made off the farm. How many other people his age, barely twenty-two, owned a farm? He would show everyone the meaning of success. However, he realized that for the next few months he would be on trial before the astute eyes of his mother-in-law, and he was determined to disprove all the misgivings that she had about him and the farm. They had purchased all the groceries which Gramp had requested and now were anxious to return to their hilltop home.

"Well here we are," Ray spoke apprehensively as he pulled in front of the Crane house. Addie and Helga stood by the front door engaged in gossip about whom they had just seen at church. Suddenly, Addie turned and walked across the street to her own house, without even acknowledging the presence of Ray and Laura.

"Come, let's go in," Helga ordered as she opened the front door. "It's stuffy today 'n' I'm getting in ta something a little more comfortable. You two kin go into the kitchen 'n' sit down 'n' wait for a moment," the mother directed.

She went into the bedroom and shortly emerged clad in a loose-fitting dress, printed in a variety of colorful flowers. The dress brought out the stoutness of the woman, who was in her middle forties. Her large double chin made her look even older. She had a long thin nose set off by raging eyebrows that met nearly in the middle of her brow. Her hair, neatly trimmed, contained gray streaks. Unlike her daughter, she was a tall imposing woman who never went unnoticed. She had a habit of rapping, with her knuckles, on any object in reach, when she had something serious to say.

"Shall I help you, Mom?" Laura asked.

"No, I'm just putting together a salad 'n' some sandwiches. Uncle John can't make it in today. He had to take a load down to Lake City. You two kin sit in the living room while I git things together."

Uncle John was Helga Crane's younger bachelor brother who owned a truck line. He had three tractor-trailers used primarily to haul finished lumber from the saw-mill to various parts of the state. He had a good business and soon planned to buy another truck. John was out of town a lot since the long hauls demanded that he spend a night or two on the road. After Laura's father died, the uncle took a liking to his niece and treated her like a daughter.

"Is Ed comin' over today?" Ray asked.

"No, he promised to take the kids on a picnic to Statue Rock Park," Laura responded. "We'll have to go on picnics next summer like we used to before you went away. Remember the fun we had?"

"Yes, we'll see. How is the hardware business? Ya know we'll have ta buy some tools. I was hopin' ta talk to him ta see what he carries."

"They'll be up to visit us soon and you can talk to him then," Laura answered.

They heard the rattling of china and the ringing of silver as the mother set the table. The aroma of coffee soon drifted into the living room, and a few minutes later the mother called to them to eat.

Helga Crane had set a table consisting of a simple garden salad, salami sandwiches, dill pickles, potato chips, and coffee.

"I didn't have time to make a big meal today," she spoke motioning them to their places. "But I'll have ya all down some evening for pork chops." She filled their cups with coffee, and then they all began to eat sandwiches.

"I s'pose you just about got everything pieced together up there on the hill and all ready to go?" A fly buzzed around the food as Helga spoke.

"Mother, you know he just got home night before last," Laura dissented.

"Well, I do have it all pieced together in my mind if that's what ya mean, and it won't be very long before I'll have everything on a pretty sound footing."

Helga tried a faint smile, "I'm just teasing." As she spoke, she took a piece of newspaper, folded it, and swatted the fly that was now sitting on the edge of the table. Then she brushed the remains onto the floor.

Ray reaching for potato chips continued, "We haven't actually moved entirely in yet ya know. But soon that place'll be a regular beehive of activity."

How do ya plan to git started?" came an inquisitive reply.

"Mother," Laura spoke dejectedly, "we don't really want to talk about those things right now. Can't we talk about something else?"

They were all silent for awhile. Ray finished his salad and took another sandwich. Helga took a pickle and bit off a huge chunk and began crunching it recklessly between her molars.

"I'll tell you exactly what I'm going to do," Ray spoke confidently. "First, I'm goin' out and buy a herd of cattle, and then I'll git all the machinery I need. Gramp says there's a lot of sales goin' on now, and I kin git cattle 'n' machinery at bargain prices. After I git my cattle bought, I'll have ta git feed for 'em. There is a little pasture left yet, but it's too late in the fall ta last much longer. I expect ta make jist a little hay. It might be better, as Gramp says, ta wait 'til spring to buy the cattle 'n' then grow my own feed. But Laura and me are anxious ta git started after the three year wait."

"I think your judgment is better than that old man's. He has never ran a farm," Helga replied. "But you know that your Uncle John says that he'll gladly give you a good job drivin' truck right here in town. I don't think you'd mind drivin' truck and the starting pay would be very good."

"It's swell of him ta offer, but Laura 'n' me want to git started. We've got somethin' up there that's all our own 'n' we've got—," Ray was cut off.

"He said he'd work you into the business. Maybe even become partners some day." Helga rapped her knuckles on the table as she spoke.

"Mother!" the daughter asserted, "You don't know how we've planned this now for two whole years. It's nice of Unk, but we have our own business on the hill and we'll get along o.k. You haven't even given us a chance yet."

They continued eating and sipping coffee. Laura and Ray glanced at one another but avoided the mother's eyes.

"I know yer against farming, but I have this all planned. I've been thinkin' it over for three years now," Ray spoke emphatically. "Nothing kin go wrong if you plan each step carefully. My parents weren't successful up there, but they never planned very much. They took each day at a time and really weren't concerned about getting' rich. I own the farm outright and there ain't one debt. Everything 'll be clear profit." Laura nodded her approval.

"Well, it's your life. I hope you know what yer doin'. There are so many farmers now losing their shirts and ending up in the poor house!" she spoke emphatically.

"Yes," Ray replied, "that's true, but they were renters. I'm an owner 'n' that makes a big difference. I realize that I'm not exactly experienced, but Grandpa has been a farmer all his life 'n' will gladly give me all the advice I need."

"Well, whatever you think then. I hope it works. From what I've heard that old man never was much of a farmer," Helga argued.

"I don't know where ya heard that from," the young man disputed. "Many people, farmers and town people, have asked him for advice."

They had nearly finished eating, and Helga just shrugged her shoulders. She offered them more coffee.

"We have ta go," Laura recommended. "We've got some shopping to do yet, and we still don't have the house arranged yet."

"Well, like I said, I'll have ya all down for supper some evening."

"Well, thank you for the lunch. We'll have all of ya up sometime after we git all settled in," Ray suggested.

"There's no rush. Git all your plans going first. I'd like to see how things look then," Helga spoke assuredly as the couple moved toward the door.

Addie Scrang watched them from a front window as they got in the car and headed for the hill.

V.

THE NEXT MORNING RAY was up by 6:30, eager to begin the task of putting his farm in order. He decided he would start the day by looking at the pastures along the Land River. As he set out, the sun was well over the hills east of Landville. From the front lawn he could see the splendor of the valley as it rolled in an easterly direction. The river, observable from his vantage point, gleamed gold-like in the early morning sun. The trees had begun to change into their fall colors. He noticed especially the bright red maples which spotted the countryside. He felt exhilarated this fall morning. He felt powerful. The world was his, and he was the master.

Along the Land River the pastures appeared in rather good condition. Although somewhat dry in places, it was green and forgeable for the most part. As he sauntered south along the stream he was entertained by the occasional croak of a frog and the soft notes of a meadowlark. The soil squished beneath his feet as he approached the bank of the stream. The gurgling water reminded him of his boyhood days where he had spent many summer afternoons swimming and fishing.

As he followed the stream south, he noticed that the line fence across the stream was in fairly good condition. He continued along the stream for a quarter mile until he came to the east–west fence line. Since nearly an hour had elapsed and Laura would have breakfast ready at eight, he decided not to follow the fence to its western extremity. He walked back up a slight grade which leveled off into a hay field. Here he would plant corn in the spring. He jogged across the field and into the farm yard. He entered the house where breakfast was waiting.

Gramp was seated at the table drinking a cup of coffee. "Well, son, how does she all look this morning?" Gramp spoke good-humoredly.

"Beautiful," Ray responded as he kissed his wife on the cheek.

"I'm talkin' about your estate," the old man uttered with a chuckle and a gleam in his eyes.

"So far, so good, but I have to check the fences through the woods yet."

"They've prob'ly been neglected the most. It's been a dog's age since anyone's been through some of that brush land. I think that's where my horses got out." Gramp looked serious. "Maybe ya kin keep an eye open fer 'em when yer in the woods today."

"I will and maybe we kin even round those critters up today if I find 'em," Ray answered.

As Ray spoke, Laura set a stack of pancakes in the middle of the table.

"I don't 'spect you'll catch 'em though. They've gone half wild now. They'll be back soon when there's nothin' to eat," Gramp dug into some pancakes when he spoke. "Shore mighty good griddles," he observed.

"Oh, this is nothing but mother's special recipe. We used to have them all the time," Laura explained.

"Yeah, eat heartily, because this is all we're eatin' 'til supper time. You and me are workin' straight through." Ray winked at Laura as he spoke.

"Don't you be surprised if I don't keep right up with ya, 'cause I think you might a got a bit flabby 'n' unconditioned in the service."

"I bet you kin still put in a good eight hours' work, Gramp," Laura suggested.

"Shucks, I'm good fer at least ten or twelve yet, and I wouldn't even work up a sweat. These are really good cakes," the old man said wiping his plate. "We ought to have 'em more often."

"It's yer turn next Gramp," Ray said.

After Ray had finished eating, he announced the plans for the rest of the day. "I'm goin' ta take inventory the remainder of the day ta see what needs ta be mended around here. Gramp, what shape are all the buildings in?"

The old man thought for awhile. "All the buildings 'cept the house need paintin' real bad. But I s'pose that could wait 'til spring. I'm puttin' a new roof on the chicken house 'n' need a little help with some of the heavy timbers. Some of the window sills in the barn need fixin' yet, an' part of the machine shed roof has collapsed."

"We'll make all the repairs this fall, even the painting," Ray spoke confidently. "I'll spend a few hours helpin' you with the roofing; then I'm headin' out to look over the rest of the land."

Grandpa had done some housekeeping on the buildings while Ray was away. But the biggest job, roofing the chicken house, he hadn't started until spring. It had blown off the first winter after Ray had gone. The few remaining chickens Grandpa housed in a barn stall.

It was late in the afternoon before the two men had laid the last of the 2 x 6's. The old man said that he wanted to lay the roof boards himself since he was handy with a hammer. Ray was hesitant in giving approval. "But be careful, Gramp. Yer not as spry as ya used ta be."

"Bah, I'm still as nimble as a squirrel," the old man boasted.

Ray started for the woods. As he reached the outskirts, he noticed the fine fall luster of the huge oaks. The fence, he wanted to investigate, ran through the middle of the woods forming the western boundary of the farm. There was heavy underbrush in the woods and movement was difficult at times with brambles and heavy undergrowth impeding forward movement. Twigs frequently snapped back against his arms and legs. Slowly, he reached the western extremities of the woods. Finally he stopped and rested on a log. Leaves drifted down around him as he became lost in thought.

Suddenly, he was startled out of his reverie by the neighing of a horse further west in the woods. He got up and moved carefully in the direction of the sound. Shortly he came upon the line fence which separated his farm from Granger's. The fence he noted had been torn down with twisted rusty wire lying on the ground or draped loosely about decaying posts. As he moved beyond the fence, he heard a pounding nearby, followed by a rustling of leaves.

He came to a small clearing in the woods and was surprised to discover the two old horses under multi-colored leaves. One horse lay on its back rolling around in a pile of newly fallen leaves, while the other one was eating leaves from a bush. Ray sneaked behind the bush and suddenly presented himself to the horse. The startled animal whinnied loudly and ran off into the woods. The other horse arose and followed the first one.

Ray, deciding to chase the animals back to his own property, circled around to the west behind them. He broke off a long twig to use as a persuader. When there was a momentary lull in the gamboling, Ray dashed into the clearing, switch held high and threatening. Ray's gestures and yells frightened the horses. They broke momentarily eastward and then swung back around him and disappeared westward into the woods.

Discouraged, Ray walked back to the line fence and decided to follow it northward to Townline Road. He followed the fence for nearly fifteen minutes noting that in many places the three strands of wire were torn down. In other places, small trees had grown in between the wires dislodging them from the posts. He realized now that it would take many weeks to put the line fence back in order.

As he continued through the brush toward Townline Road, a sense of loneliness suddenly took hold of him. For a few moments he felt lost in a terrible void surrounded by tall oak trees and a wall of underbrush. A desire to do something decisive seized him. He would hack his way out of the morass; he would fight back and gain control of this land. He thought of the past years and the struggle his parents had had upon the hill. When he was a youth he did not have to face the same problems that his parents had faced: the debts, the weather, the buildings, and, in the end, death itself. His parents did their best to make sure that he had had a life on par with the other boys of the community. Now the place was his. Now it was his responsibility to rebuild and to prove the doubters wrong. He would build something of esteem, a showplace out in the country.

The sun was dropping toward the horizon as Ray started back toward the house. He followed Townline Road until it curved around the summit. Then he cut into the woods to follow an old logging road, a shortcut to the house. Some underbrush had grown up in the road, but for the most part the route home was easy to travel. It was along this route that he had played as a boy, running among the big trees, chasing and eluding imaginary adversaries. Some of the old landmarks were still visible in the dying day: the huge rocks which he climbed to fend off the enemy, the old pine he scampered up to scout the countryside, and the little knoll topped with shrubs where he hid from gangs of thieves.

With the sun shooting its last brilliant rays over the wooded hills, Ray made a final turn in the road and saw the house, now bathed in an evening red, with the upper windows emitting a brilliant red glow. The robins were busy with their melancholy sunset songs. The evening, overcome with beauty and sadness, created a longing in Ray which he could not understand, a desire for fulfillment which was illusive.

As he drew closer to the house, he was surprised to see his wife standing in the back yard, staring down into the valley in the direction of Landville, her hair bathed in an aura of pink. Ray was suddenly overcome with a wild desire as he saw her standing there in the faltering daylight. Her features drove out the loneliness and uncertainty which had seized him. He was home, and certitude had returned.

A few leaves flew from the oaks that lined the driveway, driven now by a wind which blew from the west. When Ray was halfway up the drive, he was suddenly startled by the cries of crows. From out of the woods a flock appeared, flying low; their flapping wings created a turbulence around his head. They circled around the buildings and then headed down the valley toward Landville, cawing wildly as they went. Ray thought that he might have upset the creatures as he struggled through the woods. His wife, aroused by the commotion, looked in his direction.

"I didn't expect to see you coming back that way," she spoke as if surprised. "I wonder what's wrong with those crows?"

"I don't know. I guess they aren't used ta having so many people around," Ray answered, approaching his wife. He took her in his arms and kissed her longingly.

"I'm so glad to be out of the woods, honey. The fence is all down. There is no line at all between our land 'n' Granger's, and that's where the horses are. I'll have ta go and see Granger yet tonight."

"No, wait 'til tomorrow, dear. Looks like a storm coming out of the west."

He looked west to where his wife pointed. By now the sun had set, and the whole sky was clouded over. The wind had picked up and was now blowing in gusts. Streaks of red pierced the clouds.

"Oh, honey, it was so nice a moment ago, and you looked so pretty standing in the sunset." The young man again embraced his wife.

They walked hand in hand toward the house. By now crickets were chirping in angry profusion. Overhead in a tall oak, a robin throbbed, while far off, in the depth of the woods, a whippoorwill sent forth its evening song.

That evening around the supper table, on which a large plate of ham rested, Ray outlined his immediate plans for the farm. Occasionally a distant roll of thunder punctuated the conversation.

"Yep, we'll be goin' in full swing by the first part of April," Ray boasted. "When I git through with this place, it'll be the most modern farm for miles around. Jist wait 'n' see."

"Ya goin' ta git started right away then?" Grandpa inquired.

"Yep, tomorrow bright 'n' early, me 'n' you are goin' ta that big sale over in Kettler's Valley. I overheard yesterday at church that a whole herd's goin' ta be auctioned off. If we're lucky, maybe we kin pick up a few head, and I giss there's some new hay too. We'll have to hit every sale that comes along fer the next few weeks 'n' see what we kin come up with."

"What about the horses?" Laura asked.

"Gramp says they'll come back soon," Ray replied.

There was momentary silence, and then Gramp spoke, "I still think it'd be much better ta wait 'til spring 'fore ya go out and buy cattle 'n' feed. If ya wait 'til spring ya wouldn't hafta buy feed. Jist think of all the land where the cattle could graze. It's a chancy thing now. Ya know yer oaks are still in demand. We could cut a few and that would take us through the winter."

"I know, Gramp, but Laura 'n' I have waited long enough. We're both anxious ta git movin' now. Aren't we, hon?"

"Yes, you can't possibly feel like us, Gramp," Laura added. "You don't know just how impatient we are."

"Besides that, I was offered a good job from Laura's uncle. Helga said he could use me."

"Truckin'?" Grandpa said, surprised.

"Yes siree, and I turned it down flat because I told her we were goin' ta git started right away makin' somethin' out of this old hill."

There was more silence as all ate seriously finishing up the meal. The thunder grew louder as the storm approached. Lightning flashes lit up the valley toward Landville, and a strong wind howled through the trees surrounding the house.

"Gonna be a bad one," Grandpa reflected.

Ray, oblivious to the storm, continued, "There'll be a time when we eat a supper like this every evening. We'll have the best lookin' buildings for miles around, and I'll have the best machinery for all the field work. Laura's goin' to have the best equipped house in the county. Jist you wait and see."

"Won't that be wonderful!" Laura grew excited.

"A year from now, you'll be the envy of every woman in Landville. You already have the best house and yer gettin' the best furnishings too."

Grandpa, taken by surprise, warned, "Now you folks jist best be a little keerful. Most people have ta skimp a little at the beginnin' 'til they git well set. If ya don't you'll git yourselves into some trouble."

There was silence as Laura began to clear off the table. Finally, Ray spoke, "Oh shucks, Gramp, yer jist old-fashioned. We're living in a different world now; the times have changed. Everyone's living good, and I hear no one else complaining."

"Yes, Grandpa," Laura defended. "All the farmers around here have nice things and we will too."

Grandpa, upset, answered, "You folks don't realize that these older people've been at it fer years 'n' have worked hard for every penny they have."

"We don't plan ta throw our money around, 'n' we'll still be successful," Ray asserted. "We'll always plan carefully. That's what it takes—careful planning. Why Laura's got a real business head."

"That's right. I've always helped mother manage her affairs, and besides if things don't go right, there's always uncle's job."

"That job will never do, hon. I'm bound to this farm," Ray dissented. "The farm's mine, 'n' I intend to do somethin' about it."

"I know dearest," his wife consoled. "I know that we're going to be a huge success up here."

"Well, I ain't goin' to sit around here arguing with you folks. Jist remember though I warned ya fair enough in case somethin' goes wrong. I've given ya my ideas 'bout farming. A man's gotta be keerful on this here farm, or he's goin' ta have trouble." As he spoke a bluish-white flash illuminated the evening, followed by a loud crack of thunder. "Must a struck one of the oaks." Gramp spoke softly as he got up from the table, favoring his left hip, reached for his cane, and shuffled toward the living room door. His white hair was in twisted confusion. In his faded blue overalls, he looked very old. As he reached the door, he turned to the young couple, "Owning a lot of things is all you young people think about."

"Yeah, Gramp," Ray spoke ignoring him. "Good night now."

"'Night folks," came a reply in a somber voice.

"He's sort of upset. Maybe we should've agreed to think over what he had to say about buying cows in the spring," Laura wondered.

"No! What does he actually know about farming?" Ray paused as several loud rolls of thunder pierced the night. "He spent most of his life in the lumber business. When he wasn't lumbering he hired out to farmers by the day. I took four years of ag in high school. I've got the education, not him. We'll go out 'n' buy cows tomorrow," Ray spoke convincingly.

The wind picked up and howled through the trees and rattled the windows. Soon heavy rains came blowing in sheets in and around the buildings. Ray thought about the winds out of the west which always blew with such force on the hill. They had blown off loose boards and shingles on most of the buildings. The buildings were always in need of repair. As soon as he bought the cattle and feed, he and Gramp would start to fix the tattered buildings. When he and Laura retired that night, they both were happy. The future looked bright and promising.

VI.

The next morning Grandpa showed no signs of resentment, but, to the contrary, was in good humor.

"Shore looks like a beautiful day," Gramp observed as streaming rays of sunlight poured in through the kitchen window.

It was shortly after eight and Ray was anxious to get going. "Yes, it is. I'm goin' ta get the car ready. We will leave for Kettler's Valley in a few minutes."

"I've been outside, and ya know there's a huge limb acrost the driveway," Gramp stated. "We'll hafta saw that up before we can git through. I kin give ya a hand if ya want. Must a bin that big crack we heard."

"Good, we'll remove it right away," Ray responded quickly.

The limb had broken off one of the oaks. The men had to saw it into several sections before they could handle it. It took a half hour to complete the job.

That day and for a week after, Ray and Gramp combed the county looking at feed, machinery, and cattle. Sales were common because farmers were having a difficult time making a living off the rocky hills. The land would not allow a large enough margin of profit so that the farmer could keep his farm in the state of operation that the times demanded. Furthermore, the sons and daughters were leaving for the large urban areas where, they believed, excitement and a profitable life awaited them.

Most of the farmers were an old, hardy stock of men who had clung to the rocky hills for years. They were, like the oaks, an indomitable part of the land. But now, reluctantly, they succumbed to inflation, taxes, and land speculators. They sold out, making a neat profit in some cases, and retired to the village or followed their sons and daughters to the cities.

Grandpa had a good eye for livestock, since he had once spent a year hired out on a farm in the southern part of the state. Within a week, he had helped Ray pick a fine herd of sixteen cattle. By the time he had the herd in the Land Creek pasture, he discovered that he had spent over 12,000 dollars. He had only a few thousand left now of his and Laura's savings. He decided to wait until spring to purchase the machinery. There was an old tractor in the shed which no one would buy at the auction. This they would fix up and use for any work that might arise during the winter.

They encountered problems in purchasing feed for the cattle. There had been a drought that year and hay especially was scarce. They managed to buy some old hay in a barn that stood alone in a field. The price was high, but they had no choice. The owner had quit farming and thought he sold it at a fair price. More hay would be needed, however, before the winter ended. In the southern part of the county they bought some oats and corn at market price. The feed took 2,000 more of the fast-vanishing dollars.

Ray's herd turned out to be a very good one. He let them graze in the meadows both day and night. The grass was still rather green in large sections along the creek. If the fences had been in repair, he would have turned them loose in the woods to tear down the thick underbrush. Luckily cold weather came late that year permitting the cows to be pastured through the first week of November.

Each morning at 5:30, Ray was out of bed to milk the cows with a machine he had bought along with the herd. The milk was hauled to a cheese factory located in the eastern outskirts of Landville. The factory didn't pay as much for raw milk as the Grade A market paid, but Ray could not afford to make the necessary improvements needed for the higher grade market. By 7:30 each morning, Ray was done with the milking chores and in the house for breakfast.

The days of late fall were spent in repair of buildings and in fencing. By the middle of December, most of the buildings except for a few shingles had been repaired. Before the two men could move into the woods to repair the most damaged fence, a snow storm struck dumping huge amounts of snow throughout the woods and making the repairs impossible. Gramp suggested they wait until spring since neither man nor beast could get through the woods now.

In the latter part of November, the two old horses had come home, just as Gramp had predicted. They were now locked in a barn stall where they were fed oats and hay every night. Ray complained that they couldn't waste feed on the two old horses and that they ought to sell the worthless animals to a mink farm.

"I'll pay for their feed outa my own pocket," Gramp protested. "Wait 'til spring when plowin' and plantin' comes, you'll see how valuable they are then." That evening Gramp went into his bedroom and returned with 75 dollars which he figured would keep the horses through the winter. Ray refused saying that Gramp could work it off.

Gramp suggested that during the idle days of winter they ought to make some fence posts so that when the snow cleared up they would be ready to go into the woods and make the repairs. One day the two men shoveled a path into the woods under the tall oaks. Ray had estimated the number of fence posts needed to replace the old, rotting ones. He and Gramp then cut down some medium-sized trees from which the posts would be wedged. Wedging was an art Ray had never fully mastered although he had helped his father many times. Under Gramp's tutorage he soon became proficient. By the end of January the two men had a large pile of post-sized wood in an open field next to the barn. The wood was straight and solid and would last many years. The excess logs, they believed, would sell easily.

The next step was to sharpen the posts. For this task they asked old Fred Hibler, wood cutter and handy man, who had made money off the oaks for nearly 40 years. Old Fred lived for the past twenty years five miles west on Townline Road where he owned a 30 acre parcel of woods. Here he had built a two-room cabin and lived contentedly in his bachelordom. He could make anything out of wood, ranging from rocking chairs to huge farm houses. His talents were always in demand and the potential customer had to make reservations well in advance. Since Fred and Gramp had been buddies for over a quarter of a century, there was no trouble getting the wood cutter when needed.

One morning in early February old Fred brought his saw rig over, and the men sharpened all the posts. Old Fred spoke about the demand for oak timber now. "Lot of fancy woodwork goin' into the new houses nowadays, 'specially in the big cities now where all da rich ones live. Good grade oak's in big demand now and dat's what ya got here on da hill. If me 'n' you went into a partnership, we'd git rich, son, yes siree."

"I didn't realize oak was in such great demand again," Ray questioned.

"The profit ain't in jist ordinary timber used for buildin' hog houses and dat sort a thing. I giss dey use it to panel the inside of houses and for makin' colonial furniture and those things. Even I heard from the lumber yard dat big shots have what ya call reecreeation rooms in der house made of entire oak. Yes siree, jist let me know 'n' we'll start on some of those fine trees."

Ray looked in the direction of the woods. "Well, I'll give it some consideration."

That evening after supper Gramp was in a good mood since the goal of cutting and sharpening over 600 fence posts had been reached. For three years he had taken care of the farm, doing little worth while. Now construction work had resulted in an accumulation of material. Although he had repaired most of the hen house roof alone, it was not like making fence posts which required his skill and knowledge.

"By gosh there ain't no one kin claim to make a better fence post than me and Ray. By spring we'll have a tidy little pile on hand to sell. We ought ta start on another 600 tomorrah mornin', bright 'n' early. There's a lot of scrub oak out there takin' up too much space that we kin go to work on."

"Gramp, did ya know that there's a big demand now fer commercial timber?" Ray asked.

"I did hear that downtown the other evening from one of the Lawton boys," Gramp replied.

"Is there a lot of money in it?" Laura inquired.

"There is if ya got high grade oak like Ray's got," the old man replied.

"According to old Fred, my oak would bring a tremendous price right now. They're makin' fancy things now and I've got the trees fer it," Ray boasted. "We could use a little extra money now, too, since we're nearly out of hay and corn."

"Is oak really in demand again?" Laura asked inquisitively.

"I giss it must be 'cause they're building onto the cities all the time and tearin' down the country side ta do it. Yep, they're tearin' the heart right out of the country ta do it," Gramp protested.

Gramp was as much a part of the land as the old oaks. He didn't mind cutting down smaller trees to make fence posts or obtain lumber for immediate needs. But it was the old master pieces, the trees he had bragged about for years, that he objected to destroying. The larger the tree, the deeper his admiration of it, and the stronger his will to see it preserved.

It was the high trees in the woods near the house that had the greatest value. The diameter of many of them was over a yard. These trees were much older than the farm itself and had always been protected. At one time old Fred had offered Ray's father a large sum of money to take the trees. Even though the family could have used the money, it was Gramp who talked his son out of it. Now, again, Gramp saw that the trees were in danger and realized that it would be difficult to influence his grandson.

"Ya know how dear those trees were to yer folks, 'n' what nice shade they give 'n' the song birds they draw," Gramp pleaded.

"Gramp, you've got old ideas about trees," Ray emphasized. "The only way we'll git ahead here on the hill is by cuttin' some of the oak. The trees are my natural resource, Gramp, 'n' I see where they'll help me modernize the farm. Besides, we need money right now. We're runnin' low on feed."

"I know ya need the money," Gramp said sorrowfully, "but it's such a shame ta see 'em go. As long as I kin remember they've stood there, so proud 'n' tall, and the robins would sing there so beautifully in the evening. Now if the woods go, all God's creatures'll have ta go too. Yer stealin' the homes of all these creatures to satisfy the rich people in the city. That's the trouble with you people now. You'd rather hear brakes screechin' than robins 'n' whippoorwills a singin'. This'll be a lonely place with the woods gone."

"But, Gramp, the whole woods won't go. Jist an acre or so," Ray spoke consolingly.

"We'll have a larger front lawn, Gramp," Laura pointed out. "You and I can plant new lilacs and roses, and more trees even."

"She's right," Ray suggested. "Why the place'll look even nicer with a huge front lawn surrounded by a white picket fence. It'll be a show place. Did ya ever see a well-ta-do farm that didn't have a huge front lawn?"

Gramp looked disgusted. "I s'pose yer right; you know what is best. But you wait 'til spring again when everything is green and pretty. With that big hole in the woods you'll be sorry."

"It will look bad with all those stumps next to the house," Laura advised.

"No problem. We'll git Harvey Melvin in here with his big cat. They'll be all gone in an hour," Ray said.

"You folks know what's best," Gramp spoke slowly getting up. He grabbed his left hip as he moved toward the front door. During the winter months, his arthritic hip bothered him more and he believed that hard work was the antidote for it. "Giss I'll git a bit a frish air 'fore I go ta bed."

After he left, Laura spoke, "He's more crippled than ever this winter. Maybe we ought to make him stay inside and rest more."

"Could never do it. He's a stubborn old man. It's best ta let him have his way or he'll git more upset."

"Think he'll help you cut down those oak trees?"

"If he don't, I'll simply hire somebody else ta help."

"He's so upset about it. Couldn't you wait 'til spring? Maybe he'll be more able then."

"No, there'll be plenty of other things to do then. The work must be done now when we have time 'n' need money. I think Gramp has gotten kinda spoiled. He's so used ta livin' here by himself, he's beginning to think he runs the place. Besides if he's doesn't like what I'm doin' here, he kin stay at his house in Landville," Ray proposed.

"Darling let's change the subject," Laura declared with a big smile. A gleam had come to her eyes. "Do you remember, honey, the last time you went away when you said we'd start a family after we got settled down?"

Ray started to answer, "Ya mean yer—"

"I don't know for sure, but I think I am," Laura asserted patting her stomach. "We'd prob'ly better go down to see Doc the first thing in the morning."

The next morning the news was told to Grandpa, who said he would finish all the chores so that the couple could leave right away for Landville.

Landville had only one physician, and he was approaching 80. Doc Jones had set up practice in the village 40 years ago. Nearly everyone in Landville between the ages of ten and forty had been delivered by him. He knew both the medical and chronological histories of most families in the community. For the past ten years he hadn't performed any operations or delivered any babies because of failing eyesight. For the same reason he did not drive out into the country much anymore; the people brought their ailments to him. He simply made diagnoses and treated minor injuries and diseases. All serious cases were sent to a hospital at Lake City. Here, too, most women went to have their babies.

After examining Laura, the doctor smiled and declared, "Looks like you'll be going to Lake City in about eight months."

After getting a prescription filled at the local drugstore, the young couple drove to Helga Crane's house to announce the news.

Approaching the house, they saw one of Uncle John's big stock trucks parked in front of the house. "Unk often stops in the morning for a cup of coffee," Laura remarked, staring intently in the direction of the house.

"Oh," Ray replied. "I s'pose business is a little lax this time of the year."

Mrs. Crane guided them into the kitchen where Uncle John was seated at a small table. On the table were a coffee pot and some sweet rolls.

"We were just havin' a bite to eat before John goes out to git a load of pigs," Helga explained. "Lots of farmers selling out ya know. Can't make a go of it no more."

"Yeah, a lot of business for me now," John responded.

Uncle John was a slim hardworking man in his late thirties who had worked his way up in business. He started as a full-time driver after high school graduation. Fifteen years later, he bought out his employer who had become crippled and was anxious to sell. There were others who wanted to buy the line, but John Crane had the most money saved up and had no trouble getting the rest in a loan from the local bank. Presently, his trucking business was thriving in both Land County and in adjacent counties. He hauled milk, feed, cattle, and timber in a fleet of three trucks, all paid for he often boasted.

"Well, how are ya, lad?" John got up, grasped Ray's hand and began pumping. "I was going ta drive up ta see you, but I've been darn busy on some long hauls of timber to Lake City. Laura's prob'ly told you how busy I've been."

"Yeah, she did mention somethin' about it. I wanted ta see you too, but we've been pretty busy ourselves, gettin' the farm into tip-top shape."

"Things goin' good up there, huh?" John inquired. "It must be all of three years now since I've been up to the hill. I was trucking for your old man then. It looked kind of disordered up there."

"Everything's changed for the better. Me 'n' Gramp are fixin' up the place now. If ya went up there now, you'd see a big difference," Ray asserted.

"We didn't come to talk about the farm, Mother," Laura retorted anxiously. "We just came from Doc Jones and he said I'm going to have a baby in eight months."

For a moment, there was silence. Uncle John spoke first, "Congratulations, that'll sort of liven up the old place."

"That's real nice news. I know it's what you've been planning for. A kid will suit you just fine," proclaimed Mrs. Crane.

"And just think, Mom, you'll finally be a grandmother."

"She looks old enough, now, to have been one for ten years," John joked.

His sister ignored him and addressed Ray. "I s'pose you're lookin' for a boy so you have help later on, like all the farmers say."

"Oh, we ain't too fussy," Ray replied. "The place won't require too much help. I plan ta have it pretty much modernized in a year or so. Our children won't have ta kill themselves at work."

"Well, sounds like you have it all under control. Things must be moving nice for you. I hear you bought cattle already. I've sure been hauling a lot of livestock lately. How's the old man? I suppose he doesn't get around much anymore. I haven't seen 'im in town for a long time," John observed.

"Gramp's o.k. He's been stayin' up with us 'n' been working hard 'n' almost keeps up with me. We plan to start cuttin' down oaks tomorrow. Old Fred Hibler is goin' ta help us with the sawing. There's a big market fer good oak now."

"Thought I'd heard oak was coming back again," Uncle John wondered.

"Well, they're after good oak 'n' we've got some of the best up there, ya know," Ray boasted.

"Do you plan to cut a lot of timber? I thought maybe you'd like to truck for me a bit this winter. I'm buying another truck and'll need a new man."

"Oh, no, I won't have that kind of time. Gramp 'n' me will be workin' steady now 'til the end of March. Old Fred claims there's a big market open now in the cities with lots of fancy construction goin' on. But, we'll prob'ly use some of yer trucks later on when things start goin' full blast. We'll have stacks of wood to haul."

"Well sounds like you'll have a thriving business before long," John responded, "but, remember, my offer is always open, in case you're ever interested."

"He's paying 12.50 an hour now, too," Helga bragged. "Besides it's easy work compared with walkin' around in that snow all day dodgin' falling trees."

"Thanks for the offer, John. Well, Laura, shall we git back to the hill?"

"Yes," came the reply. "I suppose Gramp'll wonder where we are. Both of you must stop up sometime soon and see what we've done to the place. Of course we won't get a lot of the yard work done 'til spring," Laura pointed out.

They put their winter garments on, and as they left, Ray said to John, "Remember, we'll soon have big piles of lumber to haul ta town."

VII.

In order to get at the wood and have room to maneuver, Ray had to cut down two of Gramp's finest lilac bushes. The old man stood silently by as he watched the shrubs burn in a large heap along the side of the road. He felt as if part of him was burning with the bushes.

Soon, Ray, Gramp, and Fred Hibler had a large pile of fence posts piled neatly alongside the barn. They were strong and beautiful. Ray had managed to sell a large number of posts and saved what he considered adequate for spring mending. Although the snow was still too deep in the woods, Ray had managed to make repairs along the pasture fences on warmer days. Now the ground was frozen and no posts could be driven.

Ray had promised to buy Laura a television set to help her while away the long winter days and nights. There would be enough profit from logging hopefully to buy a large-screen model. Maybe, Ray had suggested, they could even get a smaller model for their bedroom.

Through February and March, Ray and old Fred and his crew chopped and hacked away at the tall, grey trees. Gramp at first boycotted the cutting, claiming his hip was paining him real bad. However, after two days he remembered his promise to Ray, that he'd earn the keep of both himself and his horses. By the end of March, they had a sizable hole in the woods next to the house. A large number of stumps were all that remained as the woods receded. When Laura lamented that the stumps looked ugly, Ray reminded her that they would easily be removed with a caterpillar.

"We'll pull out enough so that you can add about one-half acre to your front lawn. It costs money to have one of those big cats work for a few hours," Ray asserted.

After Ray's comment, Laura looked disgusted, remembering Ray's earlier promise of removing all the stumps. "Well, we'll see," Ray said to soothe her feelings.

Gramp was practical enough to realize that there would be no sense in trying to resist Ray's eager desires. The old man in a sense admired the young one's unbounded energy and determination, even though it was bent upon destroying nature for the sake of money. Gramp used his two old horses to pull heavy logs to Hibler's saw rig where the crew cut them into the appropriate sizes so that they could be carried to the Landville sawmill. Fred had an old truck which was used to carry the logs to the mill at the end of each day.

Since field work would soon begin, Ray and Fred agreed to quit logging until the following November, even though the demand for high quality oak was great. Orders came to the mill daily from throughout the Midwest for high quality lumber. From his share of the work Ray received 9,800 dollars. Gramp refused the hundred dollars offered him by the men. "Jist give me and my horses room 'n' board and we'll be satisfied," the old man declared. However, Ray gave him random access to the farm gas barrel.

Ray planned to use part of the money to buy a few more head of cattle since there were a few more sales in the immediate area. He had purchased enough feed to last well into spring from the sale of the fence posts. Since the cows were producing well, the money he had was free money to spend as he chose. After buying the cattle, he bought a used medium-sized tractor with attached plow. With the rest of the money, he acquired other machinery which would be required to do the spring planting. He forgot about buying a television set.

Spring came early that year, and Ray and Gramp spent April mending fences and putting the finishing touches on building repairs. A caterpillar had spent half an hour grading stumps out but leaving gaping holes in the ground. Within a week, Gramp had the holes filled. Grass and flowers were planted and soon the Lennox front lawn was the most gracious in the neighborhood; Laura joined in the enthusiasm and, against Ray's protests, helped Gramp paint the picket fence which had been installed earlier. Ray had had the fence made from some of his own trees. "These trees look so much better when they're made into something useful," Laura stated. Gramp merely shrugged his shoulders.

While Ray worked in the fields plowing for oats, Gramp and Laura worked on the lawn. When Gramp urged the girl to take it easy, fearing for both her and the infant, Laura insisted that she needed some exercise. They spent two days painting the fence white. Laura painted only the top portion. Gramp also planted lilac bushes outside the fence along the entire western section to hide several smaller stumps still remaining. "Some of 'em will bloom this summer yet," he proclaimed. He also dug out rose bushes from various sections near the house and replanted them in choice places in the newly acquired lawn. When he asked Ray if he could plant one or two oak trees, he was turned down.

"Why the yard is still ringed by oaks, 'n' there are still so many in the old part of the lawn," Ray answered. The old man decided not to argue for fear that Ray would cut down the largest of oaks which stood on the lawn.

After they had finished the landscaping and transplanting, all three of them were proud. "Why it looks just like the grounds you'd find around a southern plantation," Laura responded. "There's nobody for miles around who has a yard anywhere near ours."

"And nobody ever will," Ray quickly replied.

"It's the lilacs that bring out the beauty on any land," Gramp added. "Ya don't see many around anymore 'cause they're a nuisance to most people. They git in the way. But they've always been on this farm as long as I kin remember, bloomin' jist as pretty and smellin' jist as sweet every year. I can't remember a year when Ray's mother didn't cut off whole bunches of roses and lilacs and put 'em in a big vase in the middle of the kitchen table. Then the whole downstairs smelled real pretty."

By the end of May the whole farm was thriving and blooming as never before. The plateau region was blossoming forth with excellent stands of hay and oats. New life had been restored on the hill. Veteran farmers who passed by were amazed by the transformation. "Looks like he's goin' ta make that place into a real farm finally," one told Uncle John one day while John was loading pigs to take to market.

"I don't know. You can't trust that hill, but the kid's got plenty of guts ya know," John responded.

Laura still did not have a T.V. set, and the young woman used the appliances which Mrs. Lennox had used. They all were in good condition, except for the old wringer wash machine which frequently broke down and had to be repaired. Ray promised to buy a new wash machine in the fall after they again turned to the oaks. Laura agreed that if used carefully, the machine would last the summer. Ray also promised to buy a television set before the summer was over. The kitchen he promised would eventually be modernized to match the greatness of the lawn outside. This he promised would happen before Christmas. "Soon now, Hon," he proffered, "all the money comin' in will be pure profit. Then you'll have all the luxury ya ever wanted." These were words that pleased the young woman.

Spring wore into summer and the crops prospered and grew. Grandpa claimed that Ray's oat stand was the best he'd ever seen, even when compared to the oats in the fertile valley along the Land River. The alfalfa, too, was tall and at the end of June yielded an excellent harvest. The corn, a little wilted in spots, was average for the terrain.

VIII.

During the summer months Ray worked harder and longer than ever before. His day always began before 5:00 A.M. and ended after 9:00 P.M. During the last week in June there was corn to cultivate and hay to bale. A neighbor farmer, Granger, baled the hay in exchange for Ray's help: thus on some days Ray helped Granger put up his hay. It was on these days that he usually worked very late. Grandpa did his share of work. He prepared Ray's tools for milking, and sometimes harnessed the two horses and raked hay prior to the baling. There was still older, horse-drawn farm equipment in the machine shed onto which Gramp loved to hitch the horses and go to work. On warm summer days, especially, he loved to sit behind the horses high on the side-rake and watch the windrows of hay form. The old man was easy on the horses. Every two rounds he would stop under a shade tree and let the animals rest.

When late in summer, it came time to harvest both hay and oats, Ray became a dynamo of activity. He had bountiful stands of oats and hay to put in, and he owed more help to Granger for baling hay and combining oats. During the late summer days, Laura saw very little of her husband. She was able to talk to him sometimes during the half hour before they went to bed. However, then he was so tired that his only concern was sleep. During most of the summer Ray worked seven days a week, even after both Laura and Gramp protested.

"You've got to slow down and get more rest," his wife pleaded.

"Ya can't rest when there's important work ta be done," Ray countered. "Aren't ya with me? Aren't ya fer gettin' ahead?" Laura had no further complaints.

Except for cooking meals, Laura didn't have too much further to do. She frequently took strolls across the lawn, admiring the handiwork of her and Gramp. There were now various small beds of chrysanthemums and petunias, planted to balance with the roses and lilacs.

One afternoon Laura's mother drove up to investigate the showplace lawn she had heard so much about. She had been to the farm only several times, and this was before the days of prosperity. She came, noticed the change, and was pleased. She even spoke to Gramp in a friendly tone. Jokingly, Gramp asked her to move in, claiming there was a lot of room in the big house. Mrs. Crane ignored him, and then invited them all down for dinner on Sunday. She had invited them several times during the summer, but they were always too busy to take the time off. However, this time Laura consented, believing that Ray had most of the field work finished.

Laura didn't have a social life since she moved to the farm. She began to feel the strain of the long days of summer time, days of routine and weariness. She enjoyed Gramp's company when he was around the house, but their interests were singularly different. Their conversations dealt with basic, immediate things such as the weather, the woods, gardening, and the horses. Gramp, perceiving her problem, began to entertain with long stories out of the past. However, she soon lost interest.

Life was mechanical. She went through the same routine every day: preparing breakfast, cleaning house, walking in the front lawn, preparing dinner, taking a nap, calling friends, and then preparing a final meal. Evenings were the loneliest when she had to sit in the house by herself while Ray was out working and Gramp out hiking in the woods and hills. She had a radio which was always on and read a weekly newspaper from town. She wanted to get away, but Ray always took the car when he exchanged help with the neighbors. What she longed for was a new television set.

In summer, Gramp got up each day at six. He fed his chickens and horses before breakfast. After breakfast he worked in the garden hoeing and watering the vegetables. Gramp's garden produced bountifully because the old man, after years of experience, had a knack with vegetables. Throughout the summer the family had fresh peas, carrots, lettuce, radishes, and cucumbers on the table. Friends who stopped in during the summer were given a sack of fresh garden produce. Some days Gramp's time in the garden was cut short by Ray's request for help in the fields. Gramp drove the tractor to haul wagonloads of bales from the field to the barn and raked hay in preparation for baling. Whenever Gramp used his horses, he spent hours in harnessing, unharnessing, currying, combing, and caring. His personalized attention to the animals, he believed, would increase their longevity. Gramp loved country life. In the summer, especially, his home upon the hill was more than just a house.

On Saturday morning as Ray was about to dash out after hurriedly eating breakfast, Laura addressed him softly and solicitously. "Mother was here yesterday to look at the lawn; she said we're supposed to all come over after church tomorrow for dinner. You haven't been to church since early in the spring."

"Tomorrow! That's out! Granger has a lot of hay to put up tomorrow. He's mowing it this mornin'."

"We'll only be gone for a couple of hours," Laura suggested. "You'll still have plenty of time."

"It's a big field 'n' it might rain tomorrow. We can't take chances," Ray argued.

"Let's just go down for dinner, then. You'll be back for work within an hour. You'll take an hour off to eat anyway."

"Oh, I know how it is when we get there. Yer two uncles'll start braggin' about their trucks and businesses and yer mother'll take an hour ta git the table ready. We'll go down next Sunday, after all the hayin' is done."

"I know how it'll be then," Laura was getting upset. "You'll find some other excuse not to go."

Ray became irritated by his wife's persistence.

"Listen! Ya want this farm ta be a success don't ya? You ain't being very cooperative. You 'n' Gramp kin go down tomorrow. I've got important work ta do."

Gramp, who was sipping coffee, suddenly put his cup down. "Now, Ray, yer a little unreasonable. I will not eat over there unless you come too. Laura's ma has been after us all summer ta come down. Laura's always been puttin' her off knowing how busy you've been. Ya could oblige the girl once. It's not s'pose ta rain 'til Monday."

"I know what's best for all of us. So forget about me goin' ta Landville tomorrow." Ray got up from the table and strode toward the door. "I've got more important things ta do." He opened the door and quickly walked out.

Laura's eyes were watery. "I promised mother that we'd be down tomorrow. She's invited us so much."

Gramp got up and gently put his hands on her shoulders. "Don't fret now deary. You know how much of an ambitious young man Ray is. He's tired and overworked now and gits upset easy."

"I get upset easily, too. It seems he lives only to work. We don't go anywhere anymore," Laura sobbed lightly.

"Well, soon all the field work will be done 'n' you'll see a big change in the boy," Gramp spoke consolingly.

"It's not just the work. He never seems to have time or anything for me anymore. He's gone sometimes twelve hours a day. If he's not doing his own tractor work, he's over helping the neighbor. Then when he does have a few minutes of spare time, he's out admiring the land. He's forgotten me and the child. The farm is his only interest now."

"He's excited about the crops. He'll git over it soon, jist wait. I tell ya it's the good farmer that admires his crops 'n' gits excited over 'em."

"He never talks about the baby or how I'm feeling or anything. He hardly realizes that I'm pregnant. Whenever I talk to Mom, she always asks me about Ray and how we're getting along. I always lie and tell her we're both anxiously waiting."

"I think yer makin' more outa this than ya really should. Now stop yer worryin'." As he spoke he took his denim jacket off a hook. "Soon as the crops are in you'll see changes. Now stop yer worryin'." Gramp consoled her as he moved toward the door.

"When I stopped in at Mother's on Wednesday, Uncle John was there, and he told me that he had a good used television set, with a seventeen inch screen for only thirty dollars. He's going ta have it at Mother's house tomorrow for us ta look at. I was afraid to tell Ray because he'd think that was the only reason Mother wanted us down. He promised me a long time ago that he'd git me a good T.V. set."

"I never watch T.V. myself. Us old folks always got by with radios. Ray never watches T.V. either," Gramp asserted.

"But he promised me last winter that we'd have a new set in the spring. It's so lonely up here at times. I think if Ray doesn't buy the set, Uncle John plans to give it to me," she spoke sobbing slightly.

"I s'pose in yer case it's become sort of a habit with you. You should've mentioned it ta Ray 'n' maybe he'd a give ya the money to buy it. He'll prob'ly want one hisself later on in the winter when he has nothin' ta do. I know he's promised ya so much that ya haven't got yet. I think he's so excited now about his first crops that he's fergotten his promises. Why don't ya call yer mother 'n' politely tell her that you'll be down tomorrah alone 'cause Ray's got unexpected work. I'll give ya the money for the T.V. You kin say Ray gave it to ya."

"Aren't you comin' too, Gramp? You're invited too you know," Laura inquired.

"No. I always go for a walk in the woods on Sundays."

IX.

THE NEXT MORNING LAURA drove to her mother's house and together they attended church.

"I'm surprised that even you came today," Mrs. Crane spoke as they walked to the car. "I thought he always used the car when he helped out?" The older woman had on a dark blue dress and wore several items of jewelry. The jewelry consisted of an imitation pearl matching earring–necklace set and a sterling silver bracelet that jingled as she walked. Rich perfume wafted through the morning air.

"Gramp took Ray to work in his car right after chores this morning," Laura replied.

As they drove to church, Helga spoke about the insult. "He could've taken an hour off at least to eat a decent meal, especially on Sunday. Doesn't he know he's not supposed to work on Sunday? It'll be a long time before I invite him down ta eat again," she threatened.

"I know he's gotten a little stubborn lately, but I guess he knows what's best," Laura replied. "You know we've been doing pretty good lately."

"Well, you just put your foot down 'n' don't let him push ya around."

"I think as soon as the crops are all safely in he won't be so excitable," Laura suggested.

They drove up near the front of the church and parked. As they were getting out, Everett Ernst pulled in behind them.

"Hello there," Ernst greeted as they headed for the entrance. "I haven't seen you here for some time, Laura. How is it going?" He adjusted the lapel on his green tweed suit as he spoke.

"Just fine thank you," Laura replied.

"They have been working on Sundays! What do you think of that?" Mrs. Crane articulated.

The newspaper man, ignoring the question, replied, "You both look splendid today."

They walked down the aisle and took seats midway. There were not many in church this Sunday, as was typical in the summer. Helga Crane looked around to see who was present and carefully observed everyone who came in. As the bell rang announcing the beginning of services, she spoke to Ernst. "Would ya like ta join us for dinner after services today?"

Ernst shook his head negatively and whispered, "Some other time, thank you." While he spoke, the organ began playing an inspiring prelude.

After services the three walked together back to their cars.

"See ya next Sunday, Everett," Helga cheerfully mentioned.

"Bye now," Ernst spoke, waving his hand. He got into his sleek sports car, and with one motion, started it and roared away.

"Now there goes a serious, level-headed young man," Helga bragged. "Only twenty-seven and his own boss at the newspaper."

Laura remained silent as they headed toward the Crane house.

Helga had worked hard all morning, preparing the dinner, the entrée of which was her specialty, stuffed pork chops. When she got back from church, she put them in the oven and busied herself with final preparations. She bade Laura to wait in the living room for uncles Ed and John who had been invited and would soon arrive.

Ed, the youngest of the Crane children had taken over the family hardware business after the elder Cranes had passed away. It was the only hardware store in town and was a success. The store thrived primarily on the business of the farmers, the people whom both Ed and his wife snubbed when the opportunity arose. Ed looked older than his thirty-five years because of the comfortable fat which had resulted from a sedentary way of life.

Ed was married and the father of three children, ranging in age from six to nine. The store was open nine to twelve hours a day, with both husband and wife taking turns at clerking. The children, before starting school, had been farmed out to a baby-sitter during certain parts of the rush hours. The children, who tended to be ill-behaved and inconsiderate, were frequently yelled at by their mother.

Laura did not wait long before she heard a car door slam answered by a scream and several shouts. Soon there was a commotion in front of the living room door. She opened it and three children dashed in.

"Hi, Laura, we just got here!" the nine year old boy shouted sucking his thumb.

"Yes, and we're stayin' all afternoon. Are you?" the small girl asked.

"No, just a couple of hours," Laura replied.

Soon the adults appeared at the door: first John, puffing on a long cigar, followed by Ed and his wife.

"You kids behave!" the wife threatened.

"So Ray couldn't make it," John remarked.

"What's wrong with him anyway? Ed complained. "Doesn't he know the kin always get together on Sundays?"

They all took seats in silence. The children ran into the kitchen, and immediately a tumultuous protest began. The children raced back into the living room, the boy grasping a large carrot and the girl holding a stalk of celery. The six year old boy began to cry, demanding something also. The mother got up, swatted the two older children, and tore the vegetables out of their hands. The older boy, sucking his thumb, started crying and ran to his father.

"What did ya hit him for!" Ed protested and after a moment spoke to Laura, "There must be a lot of important work up there if he's too busy to eat dinner with his relatives on Sunday."

"Well he's concerned with his crops and can't take chances with the weather," Laura suggested. "We're excited about our first harvest, and Ray's awfully ambitious you know."

"There's a place where ambition ends and just plain silliness begins," Ed offered.

"Don't criticize a man because he's a little ambitious," John rebutted.

"Well, he could've gotten away for a half hour or so to eat with us, if he really wanted to," Ed's wife argued as the odor of roasting meat drifted in from the kitchen.

"But you've never been up to visit us," Laura replied. "You just don't understand what it's like trying to get started."

"Helga's been tellin' us how busy you've been, and we didn't want ta slow ya down," Ed offered. "Besides, we both work at the store six days a week, ya know."

There was silence. As the pleasant odors from the kitchen grew stronger, the children began to clamor for food.

"How soon before we eat, Helga?" Ed yelled to his sister.

"Don't git yer water hot!" came a loud reply. However, soon she appeared in the doorway and beckoned to them to take their places.

The consensus of Helga Crane and her in-laws was that Laura was being totally neglected by her husband. They believed a television set would help break the monotony of her life. They had heard from farmers who did business with them about the unyielding energy of the young farmer. Fred Hibler, buying a pair of pliers one day, had commented to Ed that Ray went home only to sleep.

Shortly after dinner, John and Ed followed Laura up to the farm. The television was a bulky console model which they had tied in the trunk of Ed's car. John accepted only twenty dollars from Laura, not realizing that it was Gramp's money.

"Maybe this'll keep him in the house now," John remarked as he put the money into his billfold.

That evening, dirty and tired, Ray came in for supper. His eyes were red and irritated from rubbing. Beads of sweat covered his dirt-covered brow, and an odor of perspiration issued from his body. He plopped down in a chair at the table while Laura finished setting the table.

"How many bales ya put up today? Gramp asked as they began to eat.

"I didn't count 'em—five hundred maybe," Ray answered sullenly. "We could've used you for drivin'."

"After my hike in the woods, I came back here and rested. I always like to rest up on Sundays. I'll work harder the rest of the week 'n' make up fer it."

"Ed and John were hoping to see you today," Laura mentioned.

"Too bad," came a drowsy reply.

"Maybe if you showed a little friendship toward them, they'd show some toward you," Laura remonstrated.

"I always try ta be friendly with 'em. I don't believe I hafta go out of my way ta be friendly with no one. Your best friends are those who will help ya get yer work done and ya help 'em in return, even on Sundays."

They continued eating in silence. "My friends aren't afraid ta shake my hand now and then, jist out of politeness," Ray added.

"You'll have to admit though," Laura spoke quietly, "that we have had good friends in Landville. The whole community has always helped each other in times of trouble."

"Yeah, I suppose," Ray spoke as he gulped down his last morsel of food. He wiped the sweat off his forehead with his handkerchief. He looked worn out, and his voice was strained when he spoke. "You two kin discuss it among yerselves. I've got more work ta do." He got up and grabbed his cap from a hook. "See ya later, friends."

"I don't know why he should be so harsh," Laura protested as he left.

"He's worked hard all day and is worked out. It's all wearin' in on him. In another week the roughest part of the summer'll be over 'n' he'll change. Jist wait 'n' see," Gramp advised.

She worried about his reaction to the television set. They had placed it in one corner of the living room. Laura had decided it would be best to have it going when he came in for the evening. Maybe the shock wouldn't be as great that way. She and Gramp were watching a variety program when Ray entered the house.

He went immediately into the living room and stared first at the set and then at Laura.

"Where the hell did ya git that thing!?"

"Today," came an ignoring answer.

"From one of yer rich uncles, I suppose," he declared.

"Yeah," she intoned, shrugging her shoulders and attempting to ignore him.

"Don't you act so cute with me. I did not give ya permission to buy that thing!"

Laura said nothing. She ignored him and continued watching the program.

"Now don't be so upset, Ray. Ya know you've been makin' promises to her since January and have ignored her. I give her the money so's she could have this here set," Gramp attempted to soothe Ray's feelings.

Ray stared angrily at Gramp for a moment. "But it's fer me ta decide these things. I'm the boss here. Whose is it? It's not a new one. We're takin' it back."

"I will be cute. It's Unk John's," she remonstrated. "I'm tired of being pushed around like a nobody. I've meekly gone along with everything you've done so far. You haven't done a thing for me that you promised," she complained.

"Is that what they fed ya today? So now they're all ganging up on me," Ray protested.

"Nobody's ganging up on you. I just want to be treated like a wife. You're ignoring me and the child."

"Oh, don't give me that rot. You've never had it so good here. Take a good look at this house sometime. You've got the best lookin' house in this part of the state and ya know it. I've jist about got everything squared away now ta really git goin', and you hafta bring in your little ideas to counteract mine. We don't have time ta watch T.V. yet," Ray ordered.

"That's all you think about, the buildings, machines and things. I'm just a thing. I fit neatly into your little scheme of things."

"Think of her side, Ray. There is long hours up here on the hill," Gramp interjected.

"I'm tired of listening to both of you. Ya think I'm doin' all of this jist fer myself? I don't know about you two, but I've got another day of hard work tomorrow, 'n' another day after that. There is no time fer me to sit around on my rear end all day," he spoke sharply.

"With yer attitude, son, ya may have some difficulties. There has ta be unity and cooperation here or yer wastin' yer time. Little problems work into big problems and soon you'll find it all ruined. There has ta be respect fer one another or it'll all come ta no stead," Gramp expostulated.

"I know what I'm doin' here. I've lived on this farm all my life, and I intend ta run it my way. First it'll be on fer a couple hours a night," he spoke pointing at the television. "Then fer three hours and then four. Next, all afternoon and then all day. The kids'll be born 'n' have their noses stickin' in it. It robs a person of his vitality. It happened ta me sometimes when I was in the service."

"But you have ta remember this girl is not used ta livin' by herself out in the country," Gramp suggested.

"He should be able to figure that out by himself," Laura added.

"We don't live that far out in the country, but that's not the point. We're farmers, and we've got work ta do. She's got work ta do. This here is a large house. There's much more that could be done around here, dusting, cleaning, and vacuuming. Mother used ta vacuum once a week. When the baby is born, there'll be even more ta do. With that T.V., she'll sit around and do nothin'.

Laura was enraged by the remarks. "Don't you talk about me that way! I'm capable of thinking for myself of what needs to be done around here! You need not tell me. From now on, I'll make my own decisions. If the T.V. goes, I'll go too!" Finishing, she ran out of the living room and up the stairs.

Gramp sat staring straight ahead. Ray broke the silence, his voice low and apologetic. "You understand me. Don't ya, Gramp? You understand what I'm workin' for. Don't ya?"

"I think I do, son. But yer approach ta this whole business might be jist a might friendlier. Now take tonight. I kin see yer point against a T.V., but ya promised her one. She's gone along with ya, so far. A woman out here in the country has got it pretty lonely, I giss. She's used ta being amongst people. Up here she's nothin' ta do most afternoons now that things seem ta be gittin' organized. It's jist plain lonely fer her. Don't ya realize that?"

"Maybe I didn't so much. We never had a T.V. set on the farm before. I giss I'll have ta git used ta it. I figured she was jist as anxious as me ta make something of this farm."

"She is. She's behind ya, but she's got ta git used ta this here life, that's all. All the farmers have T.V.'s. Even old Fred Hibler has one. This won't hurt yer plans a ta'l."

"Well, I giss I'll let her keep it. But we've got ta have discipline up here though. Discipline and courage—that's what we need up here on the hill."

The old man nodded his approval.

X.

SEPTEMBER ARRIVED. RAY HAD become silently happy. There was an inner glow in him, and he was filled with an unusual peace. The oats bins and hay lofts were teaming with the recent harvests. Not only did nature compliment him with a bountiful harvest, but friends were doing it for the same reason. Even old school friends who thought that Ray would never make it as a farmer were stopping by to admire the magnificent works.

However, Granger complained that Ray put in several loads of baled hay which were too green, and Gramp agreed. Ray merely waved the complaints off saying that he knew what was green and what was not. Besides the bales were placed on top and he would watch them.

Laura was benefiting from the new prosperity. There was new wall to wall carpeting in the living room, and a new refrigerator was contemplated. Ed had promised one to them at a good discount. The T.V. incident had blown over. Some evenings when something special was on, even Ray would watch. He never missed football games on Sunday afternoons. He sometimes received visitors on these afternoons who would help him cheer and drink beer. The golden days of September truly matched the harvest's fecundity.

Even Gramp was affected by the change on the farm. Instead of going home to Landville he frequently invited his friends up to his big front yard. The gatherings, held during the autumnal sunset, were happy occasions for the old-timers. There was color everywhere. The reds and oranges of the trees matched the twilight glow of the setting sun.

In the big front yard, which was his creation, Gramp was the center of attention. He liked to proclaim his handiwork, telling the history of trees, shrubs, and flowers. Gramp even invited Fred Hibler, the man he held partially responsible for the butchering of the mighty oaks. Another guest was old Levi Dawson, the village jack-of-all-trades whom Gramp had known for over two decades.

Most elderly people treasure a certain period in their lives which they can look back upon with great longing and admiration. In that halcyon period, they were still in control of their lives: it was a time when their worth was still appreciated, when their dignity was still honored, and when their counsel was still actively sought. Now in the twilight of their years, they sit in the dwindling sunlight, paying homage to the old times and sharing with each other the greatness that once was theirs.

Gramp had a way of putting events of the present in proper perspective. Much of what was called "modern living," he believed was tainted with artificiality in contrast with the happy years of his prime. Many people, especially the older ones, still listened to him when he talked about the verities which he had discovered through the school of experience.

Gramp had had his riotous times, had been to drunken brawls, had known many women, and had even witnessed a murder once. However Gramp learned that extravagance was the equivalent of futility. One winter when he was in his early thirties, he developed double pneumonia after a weekend of riotous spree. As he lay near death, while his elderly mother cared for him, he had time to think about life, purpose, and death. One evening as he lay in a deep fever, anguishing about his squandered life and physical deterioration, an illumination suddenly filled the room, and a brightly clad figure addressed him and told him to rise up and forsake his iniquities. He could not explain the experience satisfactorily to anyone. But after a few days when he was completely free from the pneumonia, people began to have second thoughts about his deathbed tale. Even the doctor had called his recovery a miracle.

That was the turning point in Gramp's life. Shortly after his "vision" as he called it, he got married. He settled on a run-down farm and raised his family. He ran the family like a patriarch, demanding discipline and adherence to a moral code. He drove his children to Sunday school in a small rural church where he taught a class. Punishment was swift for those who tried to circumvent his decrees.

Long since then, however, Gramp had mellowed and left the institutionalized church which he discovered was full of sham and hypocrisy. He reluctantly attended the Landville Community Church which he called a lion's den. After he stopped attending church altogether, Helga Crane pronounced the old man "a little strange."

Presently, Gramp got his inspiration in the woods where he loved to stroll during his leisure hours, especially admiring the tall trees which reached toward heaven. He respected all the flora and fauna upon the hill. He knew where to find various species of wild flowers and berries, where the rabbits nested, where the fox laired, and where fish were best caught.

Fishing was a favorite pastime for many of the old-timers in and around Landville. However, during the past year with the saw mill going full blast, they had noticed many dead fish in the Land River. There was nothing much they could do about the problem because they were old men beyond the age of retirement. The mill provided employment, and employment was more important than poisoned fish. But the men found relief in protesting among themselves. Even Hibler agreed with them in principle, but he continued to cut down trees.

"Some day when all the trees are down 'n' all the rivers are dried up, they'll wish they'd a listened to us old-timers," Gramp lamented one Saturday evening after he and his friends had congregated.

"It's a shame," Dawson added. "Back in my younger days we'd a showed 'em. We'd a been listened to. I've complained to 'em a lot that I ain't catched no more fish below the mill. They tell me ta go above the mill, but it's all fished out."

"Write to yer senator about da problem," Granger recommended. "He'll listen ta ya."

"He'll jist laugh at me like they do at the mill," Dawson lamented.

"As long as there's trees, there's goin' ta be people needin' ta make a livin', 'n' ya can't stop people from makin' a livin'," Hibler maintained.

"Let's all go to the mill 'n' carry protest signs like all those folks do on T.V." Dawson suggested.

"Ya kin leave me out," Hibler declared.

"Me too," Granger added.

"Well, it looks like it's me 'n' old Dawson then," Gramp spoke half jokingly. "Next time we meet, Levi, we'll plan our next move."

"I'll make me a big sign 'n' we kin plan our next move," Dawson concurred. "By golly we'll show 'em who dey kin push around."

"You take it easy now, Levi," Hibler counseled that evening as the men left for home.

Laura and Ray had their company, too. Many friends who never looked much at the farm before now stopped by for extended visits to admire the newly achieved success. One evening Helga Crane and John stopped in as they had done several times during the fall. Both were intently aware of the new prosperity upon the hill.

"The old place has really changed," John remarked as he looked at the freshly painted buildings in the wavering twilight.

"Yep, everything's goin' according ta schedule up here. We've worked ta make this one of the best, ya know," Ray spoke deliberately and boastfully, "'n' we're not done yet. You wait 'til next year."

"It will be a nice place to raise a family, too," Laura added.

"Sure will," the young farmer agreed. "There's nothin' like good fresh country livin' for kids."

"It'll be so modern that there won't be that much hard work for them," Laura continued.

"Oh, there'll be some work but no slave drivin' like country kids used ta go through. This farm'll be completely mechanized in a few years, yep," Ray bragged.

The shadows lengthened as they spoke. The trees to the west were much thinner now, and one could see the sun flaming through the giant forms.

"S'pose you'll be cuttin' down more oak. I hear there is still a big demand," John inquired.

"No I don't think so, not fer awhile anyway. Besides, Hibler's got his hands full over at Granger's right now. The mill'd like my oaks, but I'm not ready ta sell yet. Besides, we're makin' a good profit off the land now," Ray answered.

"Besides Grandpa's opposed to—," Laura began.

"I'm sure that makes no difference to Ray," Helga interrupted.

"Well at one time it would've made no difference one way or another, but I giss the old man is makin' me think his way a little. He's quite a thinker himself ya know. Some of his ideas aren't too bad, although he does have some weaknesses. Take them two old horses." He pointed toward the barnyard where Gramp was leading the animals through a side door. "They're over twenty years old and he insists on keeping 'em. They shoulda been shipped off to a mink farm long ago. But I giss that's the way of older people. They're old-fashioned 'n' backwards 'n' don't understand about the modern ways."

"He's been telling that old feeble-minded bum, Dawson, to start trouble at the mill," Helga Crane offered. "Why, yesterday he had the nerve to take a big sign and march around town. All the sign said was 'Dead Fish.' He's blaming the mill for everything. Most people just stood around and laughed at 'im."

"Oh Mother, Gramp isn't up ta anything. He's got better judgment than that, and Dawson isn't an old bum. He's just old and lonely. Remember how he used to pull me around in my wagon in front of the house?"

"That was just ta git a free meal, the old sponger."

"Well people should be feeling sorry for a man his age and hunched over the way he is. He must be nearly eighty-five," Laura spoke sympathetically.

"No one knows for sure how old he is," John asserted. "It seems he's been an old man as long as I kin remember."

"Prob'ly fell off a train one day and decided to stay," Ray laughed.

"Ha, ha, ha, ha. Isn't that the truth?"Helga blared. "He's been bumming off people as long as I kin remember. He and his friends are all alike."

"How can you speak like that," Laura was disgusted. "Levi has no one left to go to. It's been natural for Gramp to look after him. He's too old for work now and people mistrust him."

"Well I think he's happy in his little room above the Oakwood Tavern. He has friends he talks to every evening. They give him beer and pretzels in the tavern. His kids live in Lake City and don't seem to care about 'im anymore," John observed.

"Gramp and his friends have their own lives," Ray averred, "and they have jist a few years left, so I let them live as they please."

"I'm going ta have Gramp and his friends all up for supper some evening when I get back from the hospital," Laura proclaimed.

"I'd be just like you," Helga Crane said but spoke no more since no one would support her.

A horse whinnied in the distance as Gramp shooed it into a pasture above the barn. The other horse, which had a slight limp, he led around the side of the barn.

"He sure is fond of the horses," John muttered.

"They're his best friends," Laura smiled.

The sun had set and a warm breeze drifted from the west. The whippoorwills and crickets began harmonizing as the four of them walked toward the house. Somewhere high on the barn, a pigeon cooed.

"It's such a lovely evening," Laura murmured.

"It's always lovely up here," her husband replied.

XI.

SEPTEMBER WORE ON. DURING the last week of September Laura went to Lake City and delivered a son. A crib was purchased and placed in the upstairs bedroom. Laura coddled over the child day after day. Ray reproached her for spending too much time on the child.

"Let him cry a little," was his belief. Still the happiness of birth was hers.

The little boy, Ray believed, was an asset. This boy, he told everyone, would never have to suffer like he did when he was a child. The child, he bragged, would have the things which children everywhere now have. Each evening Ray took the baby in his lap for ten careful minutes and studied and talked to him. Sometimes, when the child began to cry, he immediately left it alone.

One Saturday evening in the middle of October the couple took the child down to Landville to be baptized. Ray had chosen the name Dylan for the boy. They had agreed that he would name the boys and she, the girls.

"That's not a bad name," Gramp observed, as the couple prepared to leave. "I think it's Welsh. Seems ta be I had an uncle by that name somewheres 'long the line. 'Dylan Lennox'," he spoke the name to himself. "If yer parents were alive, they'd go fer that name. Yes, siree, good Welsh."

"I think Ray has chosen well," Laura added.

"It's different, unique. We want him ta grow up more than jist average," the husband declared.

That evening Grandpa Lennox had a little get-together with many of his old friends on the Lennox backyard. Cooler weather would soon set in, so Gramp wanted one last get-together during the fall.

It was a beautiful evening as the old-timers gathered on the chairs on the newly mowed lawn. The tall oaks which lined the driveway stood in dark reddish hues in the fading light. A squirrel chattered from the heights of one of them. Flocks of blackbirds flew in and out of the woods in preparation to traveling south. From the pasture came the occasional bellow of a cow. It was a soft evening with dew glistening in the grass. As the light grew dimmer, the sounds ceased except for the crickets whose chirping challenged the laughter and voices of the old men.

Hibler had arrived before Ray and Laura left for Landville. He brought a bottle of home-made wine with him. Against Laura's wishes, Ray gladly had drunk a small glass of it in celebration of the christening.

"No one turns down Hibler's great wine," Ray avowed. Hibler's wild grape wine was in demand throughout the Landville area. "Besides," Ray continued, "this is a very important evening." Gramp and Hibler readily agreed.

Five old men sat in the shadows discussing the past, the present, and the future. The evening had progressed to that point where they were in the present. The wine was all gone. Each had had two glasses, and Hibler promised to bring more next week. Old Levi Dawson had become rather talkative and cheerful after his two glasses.

"Yis siree," Levi began, "people might call me a bum 'n' tramp, but I've had no 'plaints 'bout m' life. I cain't but remember my mama. It's so long 'go in Iowā. I don't even know if I have relatives down that away no more. Don't kere I reckon. My children have forgotten me. Giss they think I'm dead. But I've always bin happy. There hain't a day gone by but what I had some happiness. I've always had ma good friends, no matter where I ended."

"It's good friends what count. Good friends, that's what makes life worthwhile," Gramp added.

"Yis siree, I've always had ma friends. Most of 'em were gud ta me," Dawson spoke absentmindedly.

"It seems," Hibler observed, "when I was a young man haulin' logs with horse and wagon, friends were different than now. We could always count on each other ta lend a hand when someone had trouble. We knew each other's problems 'n' cared. Do we still give each other a hand like we used ta?"

"Shore we do," Granger answered. "Us farmers all help each other out all da time, ya know. I help Ray 'n' he helps me. Ray helps Hibler. I help old man Atkins, 'n' there's a poor fellah who needs the help. His four big strong boys all left 'im—moved to the city lock, stock, 'n' barrel."

"Ja, but helfing not alvays means frientship," Steinhauser, Hibler's hired hand, commented. Steinhauser had emigrated from Germany twenty years ago and was taken on almost immediately by Hibler. At the age of 68 the German had rippling muscles developed from years of heavy lumber work in the Black Forest. "Wir helfing another becuss vee neet someting von another. Dat's vy a guy muss be strong und learning upon himself to depend."

"Steinhauser's right I believe," Gramp suggested. "Years ago we helped each other 'cause we believed in people 'n' not because we wanted somethin' in return." Sounds of assent came from the other four. "Now take young Ray fer instance. He's only interested in hisself. I doubt if he has any true friends outside a few of us old-timers. His Unk John, Laura's uncle ya know, might be included as a friend. Ray depends mostly upon hisself now, 'n' knows how ta git along by hisself. Now-a-days ya got ta be that way." The listeners nodded.

"I's 85 going on 86," old Dawson spoke, "and counted most ev'ryone I ever met as a friend. Even those I got 'n fights with. I kin remember da night I smashed in Jebb Smith's nose. Why we was friends again the next day." The old man slapped his knees and chuckled.

"Ja, dat's very gut, ja," Steinhauser replied. "Peoples don't git much around ta make frients like dey used ta."

"That's yer whole problem," Gramp averred. "Folks set around 'n' watch T.V. 'n' don't think about friends no more. Why I kin remember sixty years ago when we'd harness the horses on a cold wintry night jist ta visit friends. It ain't that a way no more."

"T.V.'s more interesting than people," the practical Hibler added.

A reddish glow suddenly appeared from beyond the house. "Shore is a nice, beautiful full moon," old Dawson observed.

"But doesn't it say somewhere that all should treat one another as brothers 'n' —," Hibler suddenly jumped to his feet and ran around the house.

As Gramp turned, there was a loud crash followed by intense crackling. He jumped to his feet and saw sparks shooting into the sky. When the five of them got around the house within clear view of the barn, they saw a tongue of flame through a collapsed portion of the roof.

"Granger, run inta the house 'n' call the fire department. We'll git pails 'n' the hose out of the milkhouse." After the directions, Gramp followed by the others ran into the milkhouse. They emerged with milk pails and a waterhose. Soon a tiny but steady stream of water found its way to the fire. The crackling grew louder as the fire intensified.

A long whinny came from within the holocaust. Then Gramp remembered that a horse was locked in a downstairs pen. He opened a small side door and was met by a blast of black smoke. He held his breath, stumbled in, and unlocked the pen door. The horse, huddled in a corner with its muzzle up to a window, refused to move. Then Gramp picked up a strap and swatted the rear of the animal. It leaped about but could not find the narrow door leading to safety.

The old man, breathing heavily, found his way to the main door and slid it open. With the added circulation of air going up the chutes, the flames in the haymow roared with a new intensity. Again the old man disappeared into the smoke, and, a moment later, both man and beast ran out of the big door. Gramp collapsed along a rail fence outside the barn as the horse galloped west into the dark woods.

After a few minutes Gramp slowly got to his feet and awkwardly climbed an embankment to the upper level of the barn where Dawson and Hibler were aimlessly carrying pails of water from a big concrete tank and throwing them against the side of the burning barn. Down below, Steinhauser was still shooting a small, hapless stream of water into the fire.

Suddenly there was an explosion and boards and shingles began to rain down upon them. Flames, which were shooting through an upper door, lessened and found a new course through a hole in the roof. Sparks began to descend like bloodied snow. Eerie shadows rose and fell across the grassy spaces between the woods and the barn. Birds began to chirp as the sharp light struck their eyelids. The peaceful October evening had become a night of terror.

As the flames picked up in intensity, shooting through the hole in the roof, the smoke and heat subsided a little in the lower portion of the barn, permitting the five men to direct their futile pails of water from a little closer range through the big upstairs doors. Steinhauser was directing the hose on an outside wall now engulfed in flames. Old Levi Dawson, intoxicated by the flames, walked too far into the barn. A huge mass of burning debris fell down behind him blocking his exit. Suddenly, there was a roar as the floor collapsed and the old man disappeared. The other men screamed for him and frantically threw water at the huge flames. Hair on the men's bodies began to sear, and sparks burned through clothing. As huge timbers began to drop from the roof, the men backed away helplessly and sat down. Sirens and flashing lights were nearing the top of the hill.

XII.

LAURA AND RAY WERE having a pleasurable evening at the Crane house. Hors d'oeuvres and a bottle of champagne announced a special occasion in the Crane household. While the baby slept in a small cradle, the adults had drunk several toasts, with each succeeding toast being broadened to include more health and more success for the baby in particular and the Lennox farm in general. Happiness pervaded the evening.

"It's the first grandchild," Helga bragged, "and I wouldn't be surprised if he takes after his mother. She was a fine baby, never gave any fuss and learned easy. He hasn't fussed all evening, and he has her facial features too."

"I'd say he has Ray's mouth, though," John spoke humorously.

"The eyes and nose are Laura's though," the older woman rallied.

"Well, whosever, whatever, he's got, is all part of the Lennox farm now. You jist watch that boy grow into a strapper," Ray boasted. "He's gonna be a fullback, no, a quarterback; he's got brains."

"I'll buy 'im a football tomorrow," John teased, "and we'll have a scrimmage."

"He's a farmer, though, don't forget. I'm gonna buy Granger out someday, 'n' we'll really have a big operation then. We'll own the whole damn hill then plus a valley or two. Why Granger's land runs nearly all the way ta Fall

River. That'll be a tremendous spread," Ray proclaimed. "Someday," he continued, "there's gonna be a huge oak sign right up over the entrance to the drive and it'll say, 'Ray Lennox and Son,' or 'Sons' maybe—who knows what the old gal will have on hand by then."

"Yeah let's toast that," John exclaimed, holding his glass high. He and Ray clanked their glasses and swallowed their drinks. John poured another drink.

"This is the night for celebrating. Your first grandchild, Mother." While Laura spoke, sirens pierced the night.

"They're comin' after us now ta escort us home," Ray joked.

"Something must be burning down. I wonder what caught on fire this time of the day." John moved toward the door as he spoke.

"Granger's outhouse!" Ray laughed at his own joke and followed John through the door. From the front of the house, they could see a reddish glow over the western part of the village.

"It's from the direction of the sawmill," Ray observed.

"No, I believe it's beyond, up in the woods someplace," John answered. The women joined the men and all stared somberly at the gigantic red glow in the western sky.

They ran behind the house and climbed halfway up a hill. Now they could see a conflagration consuming the evening calm. The whole valley was cast in a reddish hue. The roofs of various buildings were distinguishable in the night. Even the silver cross on top of the Community Church emitted a red glow. There was much shouting and dashing about as villagers got into their cars and drove out of town toward the hills.

"It looks like my farm! Something's on fire! It's on my farm!" Ray screamed as he dashed down the hill followed by John. At the bottom of the hill he met Laura and Helga who were beginning the climb. "A fire! My farm!" he gasped as he raced for his car.

The conflagration was like a huge beacon guiding people from the valley to the hill. A steady stream of lights crawled up the hill toward the flames. By the time Ray and John approached the farm, they were stopped in a string of traffic. Ray jumped out and ran toward the burning building. The farm yard was filled with a confusion of running and shouting. The two fire trucks sprayed waves of water into the burning mass. But the angry flames swallowed the water effortlessly. Soon the sounds of more sirens announced the arrival of more fire trucks from a neighboring village.

Ray, urging the firemen on, behaved like a man possessed. He screamed for more pressure from the hoses. He tried to wrench a hose from a group of men, claiming that the water was being directed in the wrong place. Gramp, deeply exhausted and doubly saddened, sat in a shock-like state next to Hibler on logs at the edge of the woods. They saw Granger and Steinhauser pointing to the place where Dawson was last seen. Two firemen tried to work their way in but were driven back. When Ray was told about the tragedy, he glanced toward the burnt-out doorway and then continued, undaunted, in his attempts at saving part of the barn.

A horse whinnied in the woods behind Gramp. Turning, he saw a dark form, its eyes reflecting the flames. Gramp slowly stood, and the form vanished.

Suddenly a brisk wind whistled through the trees out of the west sending sparks and small bits of burning debris toward Landville. Some of the debris descended upon the roofs of the nearby corncrib and chicken house which began to smoke and then glow. A nearby fire truck shot a heavy stream of water at the two buildings, creating a turbulence of flying boards and shingles.

The firemen worked through the night attempting to contain the fire. Many people left after discovering that any attempts to save the barn would be futile. As the flames subsided, the crowd of people who stood in the field along the road dwindled.

There was a shortage of water on the hill. The pressure pump which Ray's father had installed years ago was unable to feed the hungry fire trucks. The trucks took turns rushing down the hill to the Land River to replenish their supply. John rode back with one of the trucks after realizing that the situation was hopeless. He found Laura in the living room of her mother's house. Helga Crane and Addie Scrang had climbed the hill to watch the fire.

"Looks like Ray has lost quite a bit," he solemnly told Laura. She gasped and tears soon rolled down her cheeks.

"Remember, he can come to work for me whenever he wants to. I'll give him top wages like I promised before," he tried to console his niece.

"I just don't know why it happened to us," she rocked little Dylan in her arms as she spoke.

XIII.

WHEN THE FIRST STREAKS of dawn appeared, the flames had run their course. And then the sun shot its rays on a sullen scene: a dark, twisted, skeletal wasteland which emitted now and then a muffled pop or a weak hiss as steam escaped from the bowels of the ruin. A musty burnt-out smell enveloped the top of the hill. There was only one fire truck left now. Several firemen cautiously worked through the murky conglomeration, pointing torrents of water on tiny pockets of flame. Ray worked feverishly with a hammer and crowbar salvaging small boards, timbers, and nails. He threw them haphazardly along the foundation of the barn where the once neatly stacked fenceposts now lay charred and in ruins.

Earlier in the morning, firemen searching through the debris located the body of old Levi Dawson under a pile of soggy half-burnt hay in front of the stanchions. Since the body was not badly burned, the firemen believed the old man was killed when he struck the concrete floor after falling through a hole in the floor above. Gramp watched silently as his timeless friend was borne away.

When the sun's full rays flushed the morning sky, Gramp Lennox was seated alone on the log. The morning song of birds was interrupted by the constant thud of a hammer. Where once the beautiful red barn had stood, gray smoke now spewed forth from piles of charred wood and half-burned mounds of hay like little volcanoes now in a state of remission. In addition the roof of the chicken house was badly damaged. Broken slats hung from the corncrib and piles of corn lay in the grass. Chickens roamed around the pile, scratching and pecking. Gramp slowly got up and limped toward the barn. His left hip pained him so that he could scarcely move. During the confusion he had lost his cane, and now a stick took its place. Other men congregated around Ray who was busy pulling nails out of a piece of charred board.

"There's no use to salvage all that lumber, Ray," one of the firemen spoke.

"We'll all pitch in 'n' help you build a new barn," another promised.

"Sure, you've got lots of oak on hand. We'll have another barn up before snow flies," a third spoke. All nodded approval. The young farmer remained silent.

Most of the volunteer firemen were from Landville and were friends of Ray. He had gone to school with many of them. He listened carefully to their expressions of sympathy. Hibler and Granger looked at the ruins and at Ray and then back to the ruins again. Finally, Gramp explained how he and his friends had been talking—how they saw the glow and heard the crashing noise—and how they tried to extinguish the fire. And again about the death of old Levi Dawson. In a broken voice Gramp said that he was responsible for Dawson's death.

"I shid of knowed better. I shid of kept that old man away from the barn," Gramp spoke bitterly.

"If yer ta blame we're all ta blame, 'cause you couldn't 've stopped him, nor could ya of stopped me, or any of us," Granger consoled.

"Ja, dat's right, ve ist all ta blame if you are," Steinhauser replied.

The conversation changed to the cause of the fire. Some of the farmers ventured that maybe Ray harvested hay a little too green. Granger suggested that some of Ray's hay could have dried a little longer. Besides, the flames were first observed in that part of the barn. This Ray vehemently denied saying he knew how to make hay; he had been haying since he was a kid. Another theory was that the electrical system had shorted somewhere. Gramp could not remember when the last electrical repairs had been made in the barn. Ray quieted the talk by saying that he had his own theories of how the fire started. When questioned, he refused to answer. The fire remained a topic of conversation and speculation for many days.

John had brought Laura, the child, and Helga Crane to the farm shortly after the body of Dawson was removed. The two women prepared breakfast for the remaining workers. The men ate their bacon and eggs hungrily since they had worked most of the night. Ray was still working out among the ruins.

"Well, I giss you can be thankful this thing didn't happen during the winter when ya might have lost all yer livestock too," a fireman suggested.

"We're thankful to Granger and all you guys who helped us," Laura added quietly. Granger had promised to let Ray milk his cows at his barn, both morning and night.

"He'd better sell out now!" Helga interjected.

While they were eating, Ray entered, his face and clothing black with soot and ashes. He cleaned his face and hands and took a place at the table.

"Thank goodness it's Sunday today," one of the firemen observed. "I'll be able to sleep all day now. Boy that sure was a scorcher."

"You had full insurance didn't ya, Ray?" someone asked.

Ray eating hurriedly grunted an affirmation. They ate in silence for awhile. Gramp asked if anyone had seen his cane. No one could remember. The old man slowly got up, grabbing the back of a chair to aid him. "Well, I've got ta look for it."

Laura got up and helped him, seeing his plight. "Gramp you're in no condition to go back out. You shouldn't 've been out all night in that air. If I were here you would've come in. You go in and get some sleep. I'll go out and look for your cane."

The old man agreed but said he still had to find his horses. "Don't worry about your horses now. You get some sleep," a fireman commanded.

"Maybe so," the old man muttered as he sat on the bench along the wall. "Let me rest here fer a minute."

The firemen began to leave, and Ray spoke to them gloomily, "Thanks guys; I don't know how I kin repay."

"That's our job," one offered.

"Remember, we'll pitch in if ya want to rebuild," another said.

"I'll be rebuilding. Thanks again," Ray asserted.

Helga Crane stared incredulously at Ray. She was about to speak, but Ray began, "Well, I'll have ta hurry 'cause I still have the cows ta milk." He gobbled down a final piece of toast followed by a quick swig of coffee.

"Granger said he'd milk your cows," John affirmed.

"He's too tired ta do much of anything. I've gotta go," he got up and headed toward the door.

"Wait a second," Helga Crane commanded. "We ought ta talk about this fire first. You ought ta sell out and go into partnership with John since half of yer buildings are gone."

"I'm rebuilding," Ray replied. "The insurance money will cover most of it. I'm not quittin' now. That's the coward's way out." He opened the door and quickly left.

"Somebody's goin' to have to talk some sense into that kid," Helga spoke angrily rapping the table as she spoke. "How does he expect ta raise a family up here without buildings? He's a fool if he doesn't take John's trucking offer now. Why he could sell out right now and buy a nice house down in Landville. You kin all stay at my place until ya git settled down," she looked intently at Laura.

Hibler and Steinhauser prepared to leave saying that they had some logs to saw up before going to bed.

"Ja, vat happen here ist bat, aber I helpf rebuilt ven Ray vants dat." Bidding good morning Steinhauser left.

"Rebuild! How can that old man help?" Helga declared.

"Ray's had a lot of offers of help already," John said.

"Now what's so bad about rebuilding," Hibler spoke. "Steinhauser's a good carpenter, and I ain't so bad myself. Both of us have built many barns in our day. Ray has asked me 'n' I'm goin' ta help."

"And what do you think?" Helga turned to Gramp who sat back against the wall, pale and silent, listening to it all. His hair was disheveled and his eyes were red and watery.

"I don't know," the old man spoke wearily. "He loves the land and his callin' is here. It's difficult fer a young man without much backin' ta really git started. But you folks don't 'preciate the will in that boy. I've knowed 'im all my life, 'n' it's hard ta stop 'im once he's set his mind on somethin'."

"Well, someone should talk to 'im and convince 'im. I've never seen such stubbornness. I just can't see my daughter and baby living up here on this forsaken hill with nothing ta look forward to, only years of hard work," Helga again rapped the table to emphasize words.

"Are ya sure you don't want ta go to bed Gramp?" Laura coaxed.

"He's got all the resources on hand here to build a nice, modern hip-roofed barn," Hibler argued.

"I giss I'll go now. I'm so tired," Gramp got up from the bench aided by Laura who led him from the kitchen into the living room. He grasped his left hip and muttered something about horses as he was led away.

"Why don't they put 'im away in an old folks' home," Helga observed.

XIV.

OLD LEVI DAWSON WAS buried in the Landville Cemetery in a side plot reserved for the poor and the anonymous. The cemetery was on a gently rolling hill overlooking the Land River. None of the old man's children appeared at the funeral. Only a few of the old-timer's longtime friends came to see him laid to rest.

The villagers were very sympathetic with Ray, and many offered to help him rebuild. The damage was more extensive than originally thought. In addition to the corncrib and chicken house being damaged, the house had blistered paint on the south side. Also the white picket fence had been damaged along the driveway where the many cars had parked. After conferring with Hibler, Ray told his friends that in two weeks enough lumber would be cut to begin construction.

Meanwhile Ray began the work of cleaning the debris up out of the old foundation, cutting lumber for the new barn, and each day attending to the cattle. He put in Herculean days of work. He arose each day at 4:30 and worked sometimes until ten in the evening. He had to drive his herd of cattle each day over a half mile through heavily wooded fields so that they could be milked in Granger's barn. They had planned a route so that the two herds would not become mixed.

It took about four days to clean the debris out of the old foundation. Ray worked steadily, taking off a few minutes at noon and in the evening to eat. He installed floodlights near the construction site so that he could work well into the night. Long after Laura and Gramp had gone to bed, they could hear him pounding and breaking. Hibler and Granger came over a few hours each day to give Ray a hand. They tried to convince the young man to slacken his pace by assuring him that the new barn would be constructed before cold weather came.

Gramp had improved after a few days' rest and had retrieved the two old horses from the woods where they had fled during the fire. He had no trouble capturing them. He carried a large pail of oats with him, and they came to him eagerly. Gramp placed the horses in the machine shed which was located on the outer fringes of the woods, far enough from the construction site to escape harm. Various sets of old harness hung about the shed—old and worn harness that Gramp had used long before Ray's time. Gramp bought some feed for the horses and placed it in a corner of the shed where the roof was still sturdy.

One afternoon as the men were carrying the last of the debris away, they were surprised to see Gramp driving the team of old horses and pulling an old wagon down the slope toward the barn. Gramp, in an old straw hat and blue overalls and jacket, sat twisted on a box carefully guiding the horses.

"Ya still don't look too good, Gramp. Ya shouldn't be out here," Ray spoke crisply.

"A little work never killed a man," came a sober reply. "I've gotta work if I 'spect ta stay healthy." He carefully climbed down and took a shovel from the wagon and began to work. When the wagon was filled with debris, he drove it to the road and dumped it where trucks would later pick it up.

In the late afternoon, when Gramp was returning with an empty wagon, he swung around the corner of the foundation too sharply; and one of the horses tripped over a huge pile of lumber and broken beams and fell flat on his side. Whinnying shrilly, he tried to regain his feet. He got up on his back haunches but fell flat on his side again. By the time Gramp got to the side of the stricken animal, Ray and Granger were upon the scene. One of the animal's front legs was snapped at the ankle and hung loosely attached only by sinews. A jagged bone pierced the flesh, and blood poured along the broken and twisted lumber.

"That's all right, boy. We'll git ya up. Don't worry," Gramp consoled the animal as he stroked its neck. "Easy now. We've got ta git 'im up and put a cast on 'im," Gramp shouted.

"It's a bad break," Hibler replied.

"I kin do it. I've done it before," Gramp eagerly responded.

"It'd be best ta shoot 'im. You'll never git that bone in place," Granger spoke.

"Call the veterinarian. We've got ta do somethin'. He's in pain." Gramp got under the horse's chest and began lifting, then backed away fiercely clutching his left hip. The horse made a tremendous effort to get up and collapsed, gasping. Ray ran to the house and returned with a .22 rifle. The old man limped away into the woods and waited for the shot. The men took the harness off the horse and led the live one back to its stall in the machine shed.

Again Ray and Hibler began to saw away at the forest of oaks. They continued where they had left off the previous March. The woods receded further west as the tall trees were toppled. They needed many large beams, so they worked long hours to meet the deadline they had set. Ray hoped to get the basement portion of the barn done first so he would have a place to put the cows. November was near, and they would need a place of safety in case of an early winter. The cows were still kept in the dying pastures, supplemented with feed from Granger's bins.

Ray strung lights on poles leading into the woods, permitting him to work into the night. By morning he always had a sizeable stack of split logs which were then loaded into Hibler's truck and carried to the sawmill in Landville. Much of Ray's oak timber returned to him in the form of beams; however, some of it was exchanged for pine lumber and rafters needed to build the hip-roofed barn. The finished lumber was stacked neatly along the foundation at the exact point where it would be used.

There was a beautiful Indian summer that fall. Indian summers from on top of the hill were always spectacular. One could look out over a sea of multi-color to the east and to the north. But the view to the west was marred by ranks of stumps and piles of brush. Ray was oblivious to the beauty of the season. He was like a thing foundering, but with courage and determination he was slowly gaining control. For him rebuild was the season. Work and rebuild would be his season until the end of his days.

He scarcely noticed his child during the last two weeks of October. He saw his wife only when he ate and slept. Building family harmony was not in his immediate plans. Other plans, outside of wife and baby, must be dealt with first. For Ray was in battle with the environment. He was in control and would not be controlled. In proportion as the new barn appeared, the woods disappeared. He felt more control as the days passed and plans took fruition. The fire had produced an insatiable urge in him, an urge to battle and control.

After the tragedy Gramp was sullen for over a week. He languished on the back lawn evenings and watched the setting sun. He grew thinner as languor controlled him. The days grew shorter. Destruction existed all around him. When he looked south, he saw the ruins. When he looked west, he saw the ugly gash where the woods was bleeding to death. Even the whippoorwill seemed to get further away each evening. A certain pallor hung over the oaks. He felt like talking to them, consoling them, telling them that someday there would again be huge forests of oaks covering the whole country, oaks so hard that no ax or saw would ever again bite them. He dreamed of his son who had striven so hard on the hill, only to meet with disaster. He wondered if Ray's plight would be the same.

The loneliness ate at Laura, and the desolation abetted it. She tried to remain calm and unaffected. She ate more and gained weight, she fussed over the baby, and she watched television eagerly—but something lacked. Even to her, a girl by nature who loved the outdoors, the serenity of autumn had no effect. She lost interest in what Ray was doing; she hardly noticed the demolition of the woods or the cheerful sunsets that shone brighter and brighter through the receding trees. She too was languid. She went through the motions, but the spirit was lacking.

Finally, when the first week of November arrived, huge stacks of lumber were piled alongside the barn. Most of the floor had already been laid, and Ray believed that it would take just a week to enclose the rounded roof over the foundation, if there was enough help.

On the first day that major work began on the barn, four men beside Ray turned up for work: Granger, Hibler, Steinhauser, and a fireman from Landville. They worked hard for a week and laid the floor and most of the superstructure. Ray placed the cows in the barn where new stanchions had been installed. He bought bales of hay and placed them outside the front door of the barn. The hay, he fed to the cows twice a day. The pasture had lasted longer than normal that year, but finally cold evenings had frozen it off.

The men worked hard through the first three weeks of November. Neighboring farmers came to help now since work was slack this time of the year. There had been no heavy snow yet, just flurries on several days. Under Hibler's direction, the superstructure of the barn was finally completed. It had a low-slung curved roof which would handle the fierce winds on the hill. "Another week," Ray proudly spoke one evening, "and she'll be all finished."

On a Thursday evening near the end of November a blizzard struck from the west. It came crashing through the emasculated woods with extra fury, covering with deep snow all the stumps and brush piles; it struck the newly built walls of the barn and leveled them; it knocked over the neatly stacked bales of hay and buried them.

By the next morning, the storm had abated somewhat. Between the powerful torrents, Ray could see utter destruction. Laura, also aware of the new disaster, watched him as he sat at the kitchen table with his face cupped in his hands. As he sat quietly, slowly shaking his head in disbelief, she went about the business of making breakfast. She thought to herself that surely he would give it all up now.

XV.

He sat quietly lost in thought. He was intent upon conquering the new barriers which suddenly appeared before him. He would use determination and sheer force. Discipline, power, and courage were things he understood. They had worked before.

She, too, was lost in thought as she prepared breakfast. Her appearance was unlike that of a year ago. Her hair, which needed combing, had lost its lustre. She wore an old wrinkled dress and loafers that were scuffed and worn. She became upset easily, and often unduly spanked the child. She had put on weight from nervous eating and lack of activity. She had lost faith completely in life on the farm, the way of life she had so eagerly anticipated.

She firmly believed that this would be the end of their farm existence; for certainly, they could go no further. The cattle could not be fed. Some might even be injured. Anyway, they would all have to be sold now. She knew her approach to him would have to be very humble. She must praise what he had done and what he might do yet. She knew her Uncle John would come up after the cattle as soon as the roads were opened. They would accept his job offer and move to Landville. Gramp would move permanently to his own house and be near his old friends. Ray would eventually give in to the coaxing and convincing of friends and relatives. She was hopeful as she placed the scrambled eggs and toast on the table in front of him.

"I'm not so hungry," he spoke sullenly.

"You'll have to eat to shovel a path to the barn."

"Yeah. Where's Gramp? He kin help."

"He hasn't been feeling so good. Haven't you noticed?"

"No."

"He's been getting up much later and his hip's really bothering him. He can hardly walk in the morning. His appetite isn't great either. I don't know what's wrong. He may need a doctor," Laura suggested.

"He'd never go. You know how he is." They both finished their breakfast in silence. Laura wished she had the courage to ask him or demand of him to take John's trucking job.

As she was beginning to clear the table, they heard a shuffling sound from the living room. Soon they heard the slow thud of a cane approaching the kitchen. The sound moved much slower than usual.

The old man appeared in the kitchen door. Compared to two months ago, his features were somewhat altered. He hunched low over the cane grasping it tightly. Each step seemed to be a burden. His eyes were deeply sunken in ashen-looking flesh. The old exuberance was gone; the spirit was missing. He had got thinner. The red plaid shirt hung loosely about his shoulders, and the overalls hung away from his stomach. Lately he didn't bother to put the gold watch in the bib pocket.

Laura got up to serve the old man who gestured her back to the table. He plopped himself down on the bench along the wall.

"You've got to eat something, Gramp," Laura recommended. "You look undernourished."

"I know—jist can't git the appetite. I've got me a little cold in the hip. It never lasts long. Give it a few days. I giss I'll take a cup of hot milk."

"Toast?"

"One slice please, Ma'am."

He got up and walked toward the table. "I feel a little better this mornin'. Must ah really had a big one last night. The wind was a really whippin' 'gainst the west winda." He spoke weakly and looked out the window toward the barn. The storm had subsided to a few flurries. After his eyes caught sight of the new disaster, Gramp turned slowly toward Ray. His mouth hung open in disbelief. He remained silent for awhile.

"Watcha goin' ta do now, Ray?" Gramp asked.

"Cut more wood and rebuild as soon as I kin git into the woods."

Laura's eyes opened wide as he spoke. She braced herself for a confrontation.

"How are you going to do that? You let the insurance run out, the hay's all covered, and we have very little money left. Those poor animals will starve," she spoke loudly.

"Starve, hell. I'm goin' to sell them as soon as the road clears. They wouldn't starve either. There's plenty of hay, good hay, I kin dig out. It's not all buried either. Besides, don't you worry about a damn thing. I kin handle my own affairs," he addressed her angrily.

Laura grabbed Gramp's empty cup and set it noisily on the counter.

"We're washed up and you know it. What's our income going to be if you sell the cows?" She spoke trying to maintain her dignity.

"We're washed up," he mocked. "We, we, we. Maybe you are, but I'm not. Yer always ready to give up. Yer afraid. You've got no courage. I'll borrow from the bank like everyone else does. How does that sound? I'll sell lots of oak as soon as the snow goes down a little."

"This is ridiculous! It's nonsense! You've got a family to support. What are we going to live on?" Now angered, her face was red.

"I'm sellin' oak timber. Can't you understand anything? Besides after I sell the cows there'll be plenty of money to live on. I'm not saying anymore. Yer too thickheaded to understand anything. I'm goin' out and check things."

Laura stared at him incredulously and was ready to speak, but Gramp who had been calmly listening to all spoke firmly to Ray. "Now those best oaks are practically gone—the ones that are in demand. If you 'n' Hibler are goin' ta be cuttin' wood all winter ya won't have much left by spring. You'll be workin' yerself into a pinch if ya ain't careful."

"Bah! I know what's best for us," Ray exclaimed.

Gramp continued, "Ya hafta be fair to the girl. Now yer Uncle John still holds that job open fer ya. Ya kin sell the farm in the spring. There'll always be buyers. Yer clear now. Ya could build a real nice home in town and even have it all paid for." He pointed eastward toward the village as he spoke.

"Yes, we could have a nice little place at the edge of town and you'd still think we were in the country," his wife spoke eagerly.

Ray staring out at the latest calamity was determined to set things straight. "I'm never movin'. I'm rebuilding and that's it. I have the courage to face my problems. I always did, and I always will. Nothin'," he banged his fist on the table, "is goin' ta stop me. Now that's final. I was born and raised here, 'n' I'm stayin' here. Let's have no more of it!" he spoke loudly.

"Jist listen ta me for one darn minute. Yer still a greenhorn kid," Gramp was troubled. "I know it hurts ta leave the place. I know yer attached ta these here hills. Use a little common sense. Yer finished up here on the hill and ya know it." His voice started to break, yet he continued. "If ya stay yer playin' a mighty risky game. You'd have ta borrow a lot of money to rebuild and take care of yer family."

"It's my business. It's my farm. Don't you be so—"

"Listen a minute," Gramp pointed an angry finger at the young farmer. "You know blamin' well that no one has ever made a go of it on this hill, 'n' you will never make a go of it. This place is jinxed—storms, fires, drought!"

"Jinxed, phooey. This is my hill, and I like it here. I'm stayin'. You kin leave if you want ta. There's a logical explanation fer everything that ever happened up here. The barn fire? Why you and yer old wino friends. We should've checked old Dawson's blood ta see how drunk he was." Ray got to his feet, determined to leave.

"You're crazy accusing Grandfather and his friends!" Laura protested angrily.

"I'm not accusin' anyone. I jist said it's a theory of how the fire might've started. No one knows fer sure." He spoke with an air of ease, as if he had had the final say.

"Wail, if that's how ya feel, I'll pack up my things 'n' head for home. Looks like I'm wanted up here on the hill no longer." The old man spoke dreamily; his old face had taken on a momentary ruddiness. He got up and almost lost his balance, and Laura rushed to his aid. Leaning on a chair, he pointed his finger at Ray. "Yer stubborn, always were—they spoiled ya 'cause you were their only child. You haven't learned ta think straight. Some day yer goin' ta need somebody real bad 'n' there'll be no one 'round to listen to ya. You always were a little reckless with what ya said 'n' done." Gramp hobbled toward the living room.

"Did ya hear that? He's right. He knows you better than I do. You're only concerned about yourself. The baby and me don't exist anymore. The next thing I know, you'll accuse me of starting the blizzard," Laura argued.

"I can't reason with you. I've got ta git to the barn." He moved toward the door.

"No!" she shouted. "I really never knew before what kind of a person I was married to. You had such nice ways, but you were just pretending all along. Now I know exactly. I'm just a thing to you. Something ta use. You don't care about me as a wife. I'm just some tiny part of this big wild scheme you've dreamed up!"

"Nonsense, I'm not goin' ta listen to your bull." He opened the door and slowly walked out.

"You know it's true. You need someone to cook and wash clothes. Only it's better this way because you don't have to pay wages. You're milking me like you do one of your cows!"

"We'll discuss this when yer more sensible. I've got work ta do. Goodbye."

"Either you sell out or I'm leaving!" she shouted as he slammed the door.

Laura then talked softly to Gramp who had moved his rocker to look out the huge west window. He was lost in thought, and she walked over to him and placed her hands on his shoulders.

"I'm sorry, Gramp. He had no business treating you like that. He'll apologize, I'm sure."

"No need ta 'pologize. I understand the boy. When he's hurt, he's got ta take it out on someone. If it ain't me, it's gonna be you. I kin even remember when he was a kid whenever he got a lickin', he'd take it out on somethin'. Sometimes he'd throw rocks at the cows and horses, or sometimes he's hurt the dog. I understand the boy. No need ta 'pologize."

"Don't ya think you'd better lay down and rest awhile? Yer awfully pale looking yet."

"I will shortly. I'm jist lookin' out the window and thinkin' how the woods have changed during the past two years. Two winters ago there was nothin' but big solid oaks out there. They looked as nice in the winter when the woods was filled with snow. Ya could see the fine branches and powerful trunks. There never was that much deep snow 'mongst the trees. Just even, 'n' so easy ta walk. Jist look at it now—big drifts all over. Looks like mountains there where the brush is covered up. Soon they'll be nothin' but all stumps, if he goes on like he says. Look, ya kin already see the telephone poles over yonder along Line Road," he pointed. "By the time he's got the barn paid for again, the whole woods'll be gone. By spring we'll be able ta see the top of Granger's barn, 'n' that won't be much ta look at."

"But, Gramp, now you'll be able to see the sun set so much better. You always liked that so much with the robins chirping in the evening," Laura consoled.

"The trees always meant more ta me. Sunsets there'll always be, but trees are like people—they die and are gone. What are ya going ta do if he refuses ta sell out?" Gramp inquired.

"I don't know. I just don't know for sure. I know one thing though." Laura spoke firmly, "He's going to have to change his ways."

"He'd need ya. It's yer duty to stay with 'im."

"It's also his duty to treat me like a wife. He takes me too much for granted. He pays very little attention to the baby anymore. He may have to learn the hard way."

"Give 'im a little more time. After he gits things all shoveled out he'll change again. He's overexcited now. Remember how it was last summer 'til things got squared away? He'll be all right in a few weeks, 'n' then maybe ya kin reason with 'im." His voice grew weary. "I've gotta git me some rest 'n' then go 'n' feed my horse up in the machine shed. I hope he took the storm O.K. He's bin lonely lately."

"Won't it be too cold up there for him alone?"

"No, the boards are pretty good on that shed. But ya never know with that big woods half gone. It used ta hold back those strong west winds. I gave 'im two bales of hay yesterday, 'n' he'll need water today."

"You ought ta stay in bed for awhile though. Do ya think you'll need the doctor?"

"No, it's jist this cold in my hip that's got me down. I'm goin' ta rest awhile 'n' then go out 'n' help shovel."

"I'm calling Unk John now. I know he's in now because the roads are all closed. As soon as the snowplow goes he'll come up to help us. Maybe he kin talk some sense into Ray," Laura said.

Gramp started to raise himself from the chair; Laura helped him to his bed.

Ray shoveled a path to the barn after two hours' work. It was impossible to take the milk anywhere, so he threw it in a snow bank. He tried to uncover the hay which was scattered about under the snow. What he could easily unshovel he restacked in a neat pile along the barn.

He carefully surveyed the damage. Luckily the basement part of the barn received little damage, and the herd of cattle was safe. The entire superstructure, however, had blown over. Now beams and rafters lay collapsed along the east side of the barn. Many of the rafters were broken, but most of them along with all of the beams were salvageable. He would disassemble the mess, sort out all the timber, and start over from the bottom up. He would begin as soon as a road could be cleared into the woods. He knew some of the neighbors would help rebuild, but he might have to hire help this time. This would be paid for by selling oak to the sawmill. Whatever, he could work away at it slowly—all winter. With the cows gone, there'd be less work. Now he could spend most of his time in the woods.

The sun was dropping into the west when Gramp began to get dressed to shovel a path to the machine shed. Laura tried to stop him to no avail. When Ray saw the old man shoveling, he came and helped. Before they had shoveled ten feet through the drifts, the old man's hip began to pain him so that he could hardly move. He went back to the house after Ray's pleading.

It did not take Ray long to reach the machine shed which was a short distance beyond the barn. He opened the door and saw a brown hulk stretched out upon the snow-filled dirt floor. The small hole in the roof had been ripped open much wider and a mound of snow covered a portion of the shed. Hay was scattered about, one bale still intact. Ray went to the animal's head. It was hardly breathing. The eyes were wide open and glassy. The horse had evidently lain down during the night and gotten mortally sick when the snow surged in and covered its old flesh.

When Ray returned to the house he was rather subdued. He was reluctant to tell Gramp about the horse's condition.

"I'm sorry about it, Gramp. Both of yer horses gone within a month. I know how ya feel. Remember, I grew up with 'im too. Maybe we kin find another younger one for ya in the spring."

"He's old, couldn't take the weather, 'n' missed his old friend. Jist too much, couldn't take it no more. I don't feel bad. He lived a good life. Ya don't hafta git me another horse. A young one'd be too frisky for me, couldn't handle 'im. Don't know where you'd find one anyway now-a-days. Wail, I'm tired—giss I'd better rest."

The shot was not heard because the deep piles of snow muffled it.

XVI.

By the next morning the road had been cleared, and huge banks now lay along the sides of the road, in some places nearly touching the telephone lines. The plow also opened the Lennox driveway all the way to the barn. A short time later they heard the roar of a truck engine and the clanking of tire chains as John pulled in the driveway with a huge stock truck.

Several of the neighbors had agreed to keep the best cows of Ray and milk them. He was selling only the poorer and older animals. This amounted to a load of twelve head. In the spring after the barn was built and the pastures were blooming, he would go out to sales and buy more cattle. He hoped to eventually have a herd of over twenty-five.

Grandpa was ill that morning. He had developed a slight fever and stayed in bed. He complained that not since his thirties had he felt so low that he had to stay in bed all day. With his head propped up on two pillows, he could see out the west window. He complained to Laura, "I don't know how a man's 'posed ta git well with that mess out there starin' 'im in the face."

"Oh, Gramp," Laura teased, "there's lots of trees left further west."

"Not the big uns that were near the house. They're all gone."

"Why don't you plant some more?"

"You know how long it takes an oak ta git huge like that? Wail, over a hundred years I giss. You 'n' me'd never be around ta see 'em huge."

"Someone would be—little Dylan would be here when they're quite big."

"True, but I doubt if he'd be a farmer."

"If he has any common sense he won't be. There are a lot better ways of making a living. Just look at all the people moving to the cities."

"Wail, younger ones, maybe."

"I've gotta go and change Dylan. If you need me just call."

"Don't worry. I'm in good condition. I'll be better in a day or two. I'll have ta help Ray build. He'll need lots of help."

"You're going to help him after the way he's treated you? I thought you were against his building and cutting down more trees? You still want him to sell don't you?" Laura was surprised.

"That's one thing you haven't learnt about Ray. Once he makes up his mind ya can't stop 'im. I jist can't sit up here 'n' oppose 'im. I'm livin' free up here on the farm. I've gotta do somethin' ta earn my keep. That's being fair."

"Uncle John just left with the load, and he and mother are coming back this afternoon. They'll be wanting to talk to him," Laura noted.

It was just after noon dinner that Helga and John arrived on the hill. They watched Ray for a minute as he worked with hammer and wrecking bar among the mess of timbers which lay draped over one side of the barn. Ray appeared to ignore them.

"What a mess," Helga observed as she looked at the barn. The wind began whipping and whirling around the high snow banks which enveloped the front porch. "Why doesn't he shovel around the porch better? I never seen so much snow," she complained as Laura opened the kitchen door and bid them enter.

"You've got a lot more snow up here than we've got in Landville," John pointed out. "And look how dark it's getting in the west. I bet there's more on the way."

The three walked into the kitchen. Things were in disarray. The morning's breakfast dishes were still in the sink along with the dinner dishes. Winter clothes lay on the bench along the wall, instead of hanging from the pegs. In a corner near a heat register lay the baby fast asleep in a crib. Helga walked over to the child and patted his shoulder.

"How's he?" she asked still looking at the baby.

"Oh, fine. I fed him not too long ago."

"Do ya always keep 'im in the kitchen?" the older woman inquired.

"That big living room is hard to keep warm."

"I bet. How's the bedrooms upstairs?"

"Warm enough."

"I bet. What if he gits sick? How are ya going ta git him to the doctor when yer snowed in up here?" she inquired further.

"We'll manage. The plows always go down Townline Road the next day."

"It's kind of chilly in here even," Helga declared.

"Oh, Mother, it is not. It's always nice in here. We just had the door open."

"I'm surprised they're not out in the woods yet," John said.

"As soon as Hibler gets here, they'll be going out. They'll be cutting a lot more trees. They spent a couple of hours this morning shoveling a road out there. The snow is really deep where all the trees are cut down."

"Ray's oaks are still in demand at the mill. They'll take all he can bring down. I hear he can salvage a lot of the old barn timbers," John spoke thoughtfully.

"He's a nitty." Helga took her scarf off and hung it over her coat which she had hung on a peg next to Gramp's winter jacket.

"Where's the old man?"

"His hip is bothering him and he went back ta bed." Laura dropped her voice, "I've never seen him this bad before."

"What does he say about that wreck?" Helga pointed toward the barn as she spoke.

"He thinks Ray is wrong in rebuilding, but he'll go along with him."

"Go along with him! Should've known that. Both are from the same dumb family. What more would ya expect!" her voice rose.

"Shh, he'll hear you," Laura chastised and pointed toward the back bedroom.

"I don't care. I'd expect my daughter to have something better than this place. You ought ta be sensible and pack up and leave."

Laura remained silent but John broke the silence, "It's her life. Let her make her own decisions."

Helga ignored the statement. "Got married too young. I always said that. Never expected this ta work out. Letting him sweet talk ya into coming up to this God-forsaken place. Lot a people in town say the same thing."

"When I got married they all said it'd work out. Besides it wasn't Ray's fault. We've just been having bad luck. You know Ray's a hard worker. Everybody says that," Laura defended.

"Most people know that Ray is a hard worker who doesn't give in easily. It would've been hard up here on the hill even without all the bad luck." As John spoke there was a volley of raps from a hammer.

"Whose side are you on anyway?" Helga looked surprised.

"I'm not on anyone's side. I'm just willing ta help in any way I can. That's all."

"We've come up here to talk some sense into 'im. Don't you go and spoil it all now."

"Don't worry. I guess I'll go 'n' take a walk to the barn, and see how everything looks," John decided.

"I s'pose you'll go out and encourage him. You know what we came up here for."

"Don't worry about me, and I'm not choosing up sides. I'll make my offer and that will be it," John spoke quickly and left the house.

"He'll go and tell it all now," Helga lamented.

"Tell what?" Laura asked.

"Never mind."

Laura continued to work at the sink, washing dishes and putting away pots and pans. Helga first looked at the baby and then turned her attention to the damaged barn where Ray was pointing something out to John. Soon they heard the hum of a motor as Hibler drove into the driveway with a truck.

"Well, they'll be going into the woods now, and Ray will be coming in for his high boots. You'd better be careful what you say. He's awfully touchy. He's not in a good mood," Laura cautioned.

"I'm not in a good mood either. Neither are you. No one is. He's got to be brought to his senses. I'm going ta explain to him what's what," her mother answered.

"You can talk to him and still be nice."

"I'll talk the way I know how, and it will be nice."

Laura was silent and continued working at the sink. She opened drawers frequently to put things away and then quickly went to the window and looked toward the barn.

Finally, the three men came in. As they entered, they were laughing at a joke that Hibler had just told.

"That's the way it was back in those days when a woman tried to drive a team of horses," the old woodsman concluded with a giggle.

Helga Crane gave the three a cold stare, and the men became silent. Ray immediately sat down, took off his light zipper boots, and began putting on his snow pacs.

"Starting to snow a little," John broke the silence.

"I hope it doesn't get too heavy. There's a lot of work we've got ta git done today," Ray asserted.

"I got the trees marked that we want down," Hibler added.

"It'll take a lot of trees to rebuild that barn," Helga declared.

"I've got chains on the truck. We'll load as we make the cuts," Hibler went on ignoring Helga Crane.

As Ray stood up, tucked in his scarf, and picked up his gloves in preparation to leave, Helga directed her attention upon him.

"We came up here ta make an offer to you. Has John told you about it?"

Ray answered nonchalantly, pulling on his gloves. "Yes, it's a nice offer, but our future is up here on the hill."

"What offer?" Laura asked excitedly.

"Your Uncle has offered to sell your husband half of his trucking business at a very reasonable rate," Helga Crane announced.

"He can take it or leave it. No pressure from me," John added.

"It sounds like a good deal. Why we'd have our own trucks, our own business even," Laura spoke entreatingly.

"We have our own business—this here farm; besides I don't like spendin' all those long hours on the road," Ray answered.

"When you own your own business, you choose your own hours," Helga Crane rapped the top of a chair as she spoke. "Besides you wouldn't have ta get up at such ungodly hours."

"Like I told John earlier, it's no problem ta put the barn back up. He even agreed. Most of the large beams are still in good shape," Ray argued.

"Yeah, no problem at all, 'n' Steinhauser agrees with me," Hibler defended.

"We didn't come up here ta listen to you," Helga spoke sharply to Hibler and then turned to Ray. "You don't make sense to me. And where is the help you expected? I've heard it around town. They all think you're crazy ta build again. So don't expect much help, not even from your farmer friends."

"I don't care what they think, and I'll show 'em all," Ray asserted.

"I s'pose you're having fun keeping this poor girl and that child on this god-forsaken hillside!" Helga spoke angrily and her face began to flush.

"This is my home," Ray's voice began to rise. "This is our home," he pointed at Laura. "Yer tryin' ta make us leave it. This is where I was born, 'n' this is where I'll die. It'll take more than you ta stop me."

"You promised this girl everything, and what does she get? A big mess—trees gone, barn gone, cattle gone! What kind of business is this?" the mother grew vociferous. "If she had any sense she'd go too!"

"Well, folks, I'm goin' out ta check the trees we're takin' today." As he spoke, Hibler got up, quickly opened the door, and walked into a whirl of snow.

"I'm goin' too. I'm not sittin' around here arguing all day with you people," Ray began to move toward the door.

"One more moment, Ray," John pleaded. "Why don't you at least think it over for awhile? There's good money in trucking now. I just thought of something. You can still live up here on the hill and raise steers. Think of it! There's not that much work in beef cattle. Why, you could drive truck all day, and Gramp could feed the steers for you. It's not that hard. And you can still build your farm. There's a lot of farmers going into beef cattle now, and they're doing pretty good. Think it over for a few days. What ya say? And you'll still be your own boss."

Ray answered slowly and quietly, "I really appreciate yer concern, John, but I jist can't give up my plans now. I worked on 'em fer two years when I was overseas. Give me one more chance. I know I can make a go of it. Don't you understand?" He looked searchingly at John and then at

Helga. "I'm building somethin' up here. Somethin' more than jist buildings. Don't you understand, John?"

"But you must realize by now that farming usually has been a losing proposition up here in these hills, "John answered.

"Granger does O.K." Ray contested.

"He's a bachelor and has no responsibilities. Use a little reason," Helga protested.

"I am using reason, and I've had about enough of this. I've got work ta do. This is my farm, my land, my woods, 'n' I'm proud of it all. Those so-called friends of mine downtown—what do they own? Nothin' but a house and a 2x2 lot. Do you call that security or freedom?" Ray spoke loudly.

The baby began to cry and Laura picked it up, sat down in a chair, and rocked it.

"That poor kid! What a future for him," Helga insulted.

Ray, enraged, pointed his finger at his mother-in-law. "You've been tryin' to wreck this marriage all along! I see yer scheme. Yer behind it all. Alls you've been doing since I come home is condemn. I shoulda paid no attention to ya in the first place. Always tryin' to tell others what to do. Sell me half of John's business. Poor John. What does he make? No, I won't deal with him. Soon we'd be in competition with each other because I'd want my own line. That's enough. I've had enough of all this crap!"

"Listen to those dumb words. Always was a smarty pants," Helga spoke with a raspy, full voice.

"Stop this! All of you!" Laura shouted. Again the baby began to cry. Sobbing, Laura got up with the child and ran into the living room.

"Let's go! You've said more than enough." John grabbed his sister's arm and headed for the door.

"Come on," Helga responded and also headed toward the door.

"So long, sorry," John declared and slowly closed the door behind him.

Ray, alone now, stared out the window toward Landville and watched John and Helga Crane drive out of the yard. Suddenly, as if he thought of something, he started for the living room but stopped short. Then he turned, walked out, and headed toward the woods.

XVII.

Laura sat on the living room sofa and softly cried as the baby lay beside her quietly sleeping. She became lost in thought. She wouldn't leave Ray now although failure and ruin seemed imminent. She would help him one last time. She would start anew like the first summer on the farm when all went so well. These outbursts of energy she was used to. Soon it would pass, and he would pay attention to her and the baby again. No, she would not leave him. Her mother had no business interfering in their lives. Her friends in Landville might criticize her for giving into Ray's harshness. But she would not care; she would stick through it all one more time. The baby began to sniffle and she laid him in her lap. Now she wished that she had come to Ray's aid during the argument. If she had sworn allegiance to Ray and made it known that she would support him, her mother would not have been so harsh. Now an irreparable split had occurred. She would try her best to make everything work out.

Laura heard a shuffling sound in Gramp's bedroom. She wiped her eyes and waited for the old man's appearance. Soon the familiar thud of the cane was heard, and he entered the living room.

"Wail, yer shore quiet now," Gramp spoke as he slowly approached her.

"Yes, baby's sleeping now. How do you feel?"

"Oh, better. Think I'll go out 'n' git a few licks in yet today."

"It's awfully cold out, and you're still not well. You'd be better resting yet."

"Need the frish air. Say, what was that commotion I heerd awhile ago?" he cocked his head sideways quizzically.

"Oh, mom 'n' John were up here to see Ray."

"She gave 'im hell, did she?"

"Yeah, she started it. I doubt she'll come back here for awhile. She asked me ta move home."

"Watcha goin' ta do?" He gave her a determined look. She shrugged her shoulders, testing him.

"Ya know where yer duty is. I have opinions about yer mother that I won't mention. You can't run off that easily 'n' leave 'im alone."

"I'm not running off anywhere. This is my home. My home will never be in Landville again." She nuzzled the top of the baby's head. Her voice became somber as she continued, "I wonder if he'd miss us though, if baby and me left him." She spoke almost to herself.

"He'd miss ya. I know he'd miss ya. He mightn't act like it at times, but he'd miss ya alright," Gramp sat on the sofa next to her. "This whole thing seems mighty ridiculous ta me. Don't pay no attention to yer ma. Don't listen ta her. She's never liked folks up here on the hill, I giss, 'n' she didn't like ta see you marry a farmer."

"It wouldn't be her fault if it doesn't work out for us. He'd have only himself to blame," Laura avowed.

"Don'tcha think you'd be a little ta blame if somethin' like that happened?"

"No, why should I feel so bad about it if he can't treat me decent? He ignores me so much at times.

"Ya know all the bad things that have gone on up here. Ya can't blame 'im fer bein' a little nervous. But that boy's got guts. Another guy'd given up by now. He's kind of sensitive 'bout this hill, a kind a dreamer I giss. He's bound to make somethin' outa this hill. He's gotta prove somethin' I giss. Now if you stick by 'im it'll go so much better."

"What's he got to prove?" she spoke determinedly.

"Prove he's got what it takes. It's not the farm alone. There's somethin' else, but it's hard for me ta explain 'zactly." The old man thought for awhile. "Ya know how hard it was for his parents up here. They was poor. Never could make any profit up here. He saw how they struggled fer years 'n' years, 'n' then died so tragic. He might be doing it fer his parents. He wants ta build somethin' big up here. Somethin', you, yer folks, 'n' everyone kin be proud of. Nothin'll stop 'im, no sir, nothin'." Gramp spoke with an air of pride, and he seemed to stare into a distant vagueness. "Ya know what a proud lad he is. Town'd be defeat for 'im. Don't expect him ta move to Craneville. I mean Landville." A smile came to the old man's face as he mused over his mistake.

Laura was also amused by the mistake. There was silence, and a saw buzzed in the distance. She spoke slowly, "Well, he could still be defeated by this hill. And at times that's where he seems to be going."

"Long as he's got this here farm and trees, the boy will never own defeat." A chain saw continued humming as he spoke. "As long as he's alive he'll probably be cuttin' 'n' buildin'."

"Cutting and building," she echoed. "He builds something and then has to start all over again."

"Wail it ain't his fault if he has bad luck. Now if you went away, you'd jist be increasin' his bad luck." He got slowly to his feet. "Jist keep yer hopes up, honey. Soon spring'll be here again, 'n' things'll look beauteeful. We'll both go ta work on the front lawn, 'n' you jist watch the lilacs and roses grow. Can't ya jist see it all now, the white picket fence 'n' all the pretty flowers. We'll even plant gladiolas and mums where the big trees are missin'. You'll love it here in the spring when the warm days return and the sap starts flowin' again. Oh I kin feel it already." He looked dreamily out a window which overlooked the lawn. Then he turned slowly and limped toward the kitchen. "Wail, I giss I'll go out 'n' catch me a nip of frish air."

The sound of the chain saw had now ceased as they went into the kitchen, and Gramp began dressing for the outdoors.

"You don't look too well yet, Gramp," Laura protested. "Don't stay out too long."

"Nah, jist wanna look things over."

Before Gramp could leave, the door flew open and Ray stumbled in half-carrying Hibler.

"He slipped 'n' cut his hand in the saw. Help me!"

Laura and Gramp were dumbfounded by the sight they saw. Hibler's gloved left hand had been sliced into and blood drained freely onto the kitchen linoleum. Ray set the injured man on a chair. Hibler's face was pale and he urged them to do something.

"We've got to stop the bleeding," Laura yelled.

"Git a dish towel," Ray commanded. Ray broke a section off a broom handle while Laura got a dish towel. Hastily they made a tourniquet. Shortly the bleeding stopped.

"You and Gramp get him ready while I call an ambulance," Ray directed.

Laura looked at Hibler whose head had now fallen forward.

"I feel dizzy," the old woodcutter mumbled.

Both Laura and Gramp held him and consoled him. "Take it easy. The ambulance will be here real soon," Laura encouraged.

Soon a siren was heard in the valley below and became louder and louder as the ambulance approached the farm.

"Up and easy now," Ray cautioned as they moved Hibler toward the door. Laura held the tourniquet as Ray half-carried the injured man to the waiting ambulance.

Two attendants grabbed Hibler and gently laid him on a stretcher. One attendant began working on the wound while the other one drove the vehicle away.

XVIII.

Hibler was confined to a hospital in Lake City for almost two weeks. The wound was serious, for he lost the little finger and the top part of the ring finger. The wound healed well, and after the hospital stay, Ray and Laura gladly opened their home to him. He was to convalesce for a month before he could go back to work again. Although Hibler had a younger sister living in Lake City, Ray felt obligated to care for him since the accident occurred on his farm.

A bed was set up in the western end of the living room so that Hibler could receive the full benefit of the afternoon sun. The bed was across from the doorway to Gramp's room and the two old friends conversed at length.

During the first part of December, Ray, who by now had become an expert woodcutter, worked long hours alone in the woods. He cut trees down, wedged the long trunks into halves and quarters, and managed even to stack many of them. He frequently skipped dinner and quickly ate supper before going back to work. He left the farm some days to help Steinhauser on other jobs that Hibler had contracted. Laura longed for some normalcy but remembered the new commitment she had made. Even though he ignored the baby and her, she kept up hope by looking at the future and the happiness she believed existed there.

Gramp slowly got better, and before Christmas was testing his hip by shoveling paths through the snow that drifted after each flurry of wind. He never stayed out for more than an hour at a time. During a warm spell near Christmas, he went into the woods for a few hours each day to test his swing with an ax. Both Ray and Laura protested, but Hibler said no harm would be done since Gramp was just trimming smaller branches off the toppled trees using only a light ax. Soon the old farmer declared himself fit and stayed half a day at a time.

Meanwhile Laura nursed Hibler. After three weeks convalescing in the Lennox house, he felt he was ready to cut wood again. But after the doctor's recommendation Hibler decided to wait until after Christmas. However, Hibler did some work around the farmyard, the most important of which was taking stock of the salvaged timbers that Ray had stacked neatly along the foundation. He counted the various sized beams and rafters and made a blueprint of a reconstructed barn incorporating all the salvaged pieces. He was able to determine exactly what kinds of lumber would be needed to rebuild the barn.

During the last part of December a serenity prevailed throughout the household. Gramp and Hibler whiled away the long winter evenings by reminiscing. Laura set the television in the kitchen so that it would not interrupt the old men while they gossiped. At times she waited late into the evenings entertained by television and by peals of laughter from the living room.

A week before Christmas Laura set up a beautiful Christmas tree, adorned with blue lights and an apex star. It was set in the eastern end of the living room in front of a huge window. On crisp winter nights the tree could be seen from the bottom of the hill by anyone traveling the

Townline Road. John had offered to buy them a tree, but Ray, as was the custom on the farm, went out into a pine grove and chopped down his own. Many presents, some wrapped gaudily, appeared beneath the tree. A day before Christmas, John, coming after a load of timber, placed several more gifts under the tree.

This was the first Christmas in which Laura did not visit her mother. The previous year Laura and Ray had driven down in the afternoon. This year Helga Crane had called and invited Laura and the baby to spend a few days with her over the holidays. Laura had declined, saying that she had too much work ahead of her with all the men to take care of.

Christmas Eve was a pleasant time on the hill. There was an aura of togetherness and gaiety, a sharp contrast to the past few months. An air of hope permeated the Lennox household. The packages were opened amid a bustle of laughter and excitement. From the Oakwood Tavern, Ray and Gramp each got a bottle of brandy. Laura and the baby each received clothing from Helga and John, but there was nothing for Ray and Gramp from the Crane household. From Ray and Laura, Hibler and Gramp both got dark sweaters. Holding his sweater in front of him, Gramp admired it. "Ain't it nice," he boasted. Then he tried it on and held out his arms, still admiring.

Hibler's sweater was dark brown. He put his on and held his arm next to Gramp's to match the quality. "Mine's got a heavier stitch," Hibler bragged. "A better quality."

"Mine's easier on the eye," Gramp countered.

"Mine settles better 'round the shoulders," Hibler answered.

Gramp was ready to retort but was cut off by Laura. "Oh, you guys. Those sweaters are identical."

"Yeah, made by the same company. They're identical styles. Only colors are different," Ray added.

"Thank ya all very much," Hibler spoke as he caressed the wool edges.

"Yes siree, my thanks also." Then Gramp got up and went to his bedroom. They heard him rummaging around in the closet where he kept old keepsakes. Soon he appeared with two little boxes in his hands. He gave one to Ray and the other to Laura.

"Been wantin' ta give this to ya fer a year now, but last Christmas ya all run off for Landville before I could git started." Laura opened her box and was startled by a gold necklace from which hung a red stone in a locket.

"That's a januine gold chain with a januine ruby. Gave it to my wife the second year we was married. Go ahead 'n' put it on. Yes siree, those things improve with age. Jist look at it shine."

"Oh Gramp!" Laura hugged the old man. "Why are you giving such a beautiful thing to me? It's so beautiful. I won't know where ta keep it. It must be valuable. Thank you so much."

"Wail, it's a fairly nice piece of jewelry. Yes siree. I always said that a beautiful girl should have beautiful things," Gramp proclaimed.

Next, attention was focused on Ray who was holding up a gold pocket watch. He protested, "But, Gramp, this is the old watch that yer father brought from Wales."

"Shur is! That's it all right. Twenty-four caret gold. Runs a might slow now, but still runs. It's yers, my boy. A man can't take things to the grave with 'im ya know. Take off the back cover 'n' look inside."

"There's a picture," Ray said.

"Engraved, my boy; that's the old home in Wales. Some day you 'n' Laura kin go back home, 'n' you'll already know how it looks."

"Thanks a million, Gramp. Doubt if I'll git over there. I shoulda stopped in when on the way home from the service," Ray said.

"I think I still might git there some day. What ya think Fred? This summer let's me and you fly one of those big jets over."

"Well," Hibler looked at his hand.

"Even if yer hand's a little stiff won't matter. I'll help ya with yer flyin'. I've got better wings than you." Gramp laughed at his half-baked joke and immediately changed the subject, "Let's break open a bottle. I ain't felt so good in years."

The old man broke open the seal on a bottle of brandy while Laura got some glasses. After Gramp had filled them, he held his glass up and gave a Christmas toast, "I drink to a merry Christmas 'n' a happy year ahead fer everyone on the hill."

"Yeah, a happy year on the hill," they all raised their glasses and echoed Gramp.

"Poor little Dylan. Some day I'll have ta tell him about this night," Laura's voice was soft and solemn.

"Some day he'll have a tree in the same place and will be doing the same thing," Ray added.

"Yes siree," Gramp responded, "'n' you'll be here in my place." He finished his glass of brandy and poured a little more.

"By then this place'll be somethin'. Can't ya jist picture in yer mind what it'll be like up here then?" Ray mused.

They all glanced at little Dylan and had their private thoughts. The child lay peacefully asleep in a crib next to the Christmas tree. Outside, beyond the apex star a full moon reflected off the snow creating a fantasy world. Lights flickered in the distance where Landville was celebrating its Christmas. The tall oaks along the driveway cast dark shadows on the snow. A solemn hush lay across the land.

Christmas day dawned gloriously. The sun peeked over the eastern horizon and covered the land with a crimson shade. A gusty wind blew whiffs of snow across the white laden fields and rattled and whistled around the windows. The morning rays wound themselves through the Christmas tree window and fell on the little boy who slept soundly beneath the tree. The two old men had insisted that the sleeping child remain in the living room for the rest of the night. It had been after midnight when the celebration ended, and the parents regretted moving the child. Ray got up Christmas morning and looked at the sleeping baby. The sight reassured him, and he left the house humming a carol.

XIX.

In Landville on Christmas day, Helga Crane got up early to attend church. Ed Crane and his family were having dinner at her house this day. At church she saw the usual, familiar people who asked the usual, familiar questions concerning the state of affairs on the hill. She explained in her customary way that things were not going too well on the farm, that her daughter was having a rough life, that the child was frequently ill, and that the house had little heat. The parishioners would shake their heads in disbelief and feel sorry for the poor young woman who was being held a prisoner on the barren hill. Several had even asked the pastor to go up and reason with the boy. If only they could get him back in church. This would be the first step. However, the pastor argued that "God will look after His children."

Mrs. Crane walked home from services with her neighbor Mrs. Addie Scrang.

"Did ya see that Mrs. Kloten today? She's got somethin' new on every Sunday," Addie pointed out.

"She's got that high-paying office job over in Central City ya know. But she probably takes in a little on the side." Both women laughed at the apparent implication.

"Really is a snob too. Won't hardly look at me. Jist because her two kids are in college out East," Addie continued.

In the background, "Hark the Herald Angels" sounded over the loudspeakers sitting on top of the Landville State Bank. Each year a week before Christmas, the civic-minded bank president, Mr. Lawrence, personally directed the placement of the twin speaker horns, each pointing in opposite directions down Main Street. It was a feature the Landvillers had come to expect and appreciate every year.

Before Thanksgiving, the Landville merchants had strung peppermint stick ropes across the three blocks that represented the downtown business district. In the center of each rope they hung signs indicative of the Christmas spirit. Each carried a single word message: "Hope," "Peace," "Love," "Glory," "Joy," and "Mercy." For the past four years the signs had recorded the same message. However, each year they were placed in a different position, on a different rope. In the display windows along the three blocks, squeezed in among the merchandise, were more messages: "Merry Xmas," "Cheers at Xmas," and "Xmas Greetings."

"I giss we'll have to go to Central City and see what we can find," Mrs. Crane spouted.

"Ha, Gert, two old Grandmas like us."

"Well, I heard Mildred in the pew behind whisper that she might be gettin' married again."

"Don't know what she wants ta git married for. Her old man left her plenty of money," Addie concluded. "Say, is Laura comin' down today?" They were now approaching the Crane household.

"I don't believe so because I didn't want him down here spoilin' our Christmas."

"I used ta like Ray. Remember how polite he used ta be when he delivered us those fresh eggs? So much better than his parents. But now after all you've told me about 'im, don't believe I'd care much for 'im myself anymore. And ya know jist about everyone on our block feels the same about 'im. My sakes, I don't know whatever came over that boy ta make 'im so bad now. Hank 'n' me brought up all our children on a poor farm 'n' they all turned out well 'n'—"

"He's stupid. Just plain stupid 'n' stubborn. I've warned her, but she just stays up there and suffers. That stupid boy will drive her crazy before long. He's deserved everything that's happened to him," Mrs. Crane retorted.

In front of the Crane house, John was unloading sacks of groceries from his car. When he saw both of them he yelled, "Merry Christmas!"

"Merry Christmas!" Addie repeated and continued, "I had my groceries delivered last night. Havin' all the kids in today except Charlie. Can't make it from Lake City. My land, sure turned out ta be a nice day. Got everything ready ta go. Roast's in the oven. Well, call me, 'n' let me know what ya got for Christmas. Kids always give me such nice things. Got lot of stuff under the tree." Mrs. Scrang moved close to Mrs. Crane and whispered, "Think that one box is that 'lectric hair dryer I was hopin' they'd git me. Merry Christmas everyone, 'n' drop over sometime."

Helga helped John with the bags of groceries which they carried into the kitchen. "What's the big meal going ta be today?" John inquired.

"I bought a real nice duck—not too fat either. It's been roasting for over an hour already." As she spoke, she opened the oven and peeked in. The duck was sizzling and brown. A pleasant aroma of stuffing and baking meat filled the kitchen. While they were sorting out the groceries, the front door burst open and three children rushed into the house, each carrying a small present. They ran into the kitchen.

"These are for you, Auntie," the small girl indicated.

"Put them under the tree. We'll open them later. Where's mommy and daddy?" Helga asked.

All the children tried to shout at once that the parents were getting even more presents out of the trunk of the car, to which Helga replied, "Isn't that nice."

The oldest boy who had left the group ran back to the kitchen shouting, "Here they come! Here they come!"

Ed Crane, followed by his wife, came through the front door, each carrying several gaily wrapped boxes which they placed under the Christmas tree.

"Santa came last night!" the little girl shouted elatedly.

"He came right down the chimney when we were all in bed last night!" the smaller boy concurred and then looked at his older brother who pouted and began to suck his thumb.

The pile of gifts under the tree had risen to new heights. The children began stacking the gifts in pyramids until one of the piles fell over. This brought the mother who scolded them harshly, saying that they might break something. Next the children's attention was directed to a nativity scene which stood on a small stand in a corner of the living room. The little girl picked up the Virgin and examined it.

"That's Jesus," the oldest boy pointed at the Christ child lying in the manger. The mother rushed over, determined, and slapped the oldest boy on the back.

"You kids git over to that sofa and sit! No more foolin' around. Git now!"

The children marched resolutely to the sofa and sat. They spoke softly in whispers while the adults laughed and talked loudly in the kitchen where they were having the first round of cocktails.

By one o'clock the family was seated around the tables. The adults were seated at the big table in the kitchen while nearby the children were seated at a smaller table which John had brought up from the basement. The huge duck had been carved and now lay on a platter in the middle of the table. Before the dining began, Helga Crane plugged in the Christmas tree, on top of which a golden angel blinked on and off to the amusement of everyone.

"Where did you get that?" Ed inquired.

"Down at Hold's Dime Store. Me 'n' Addie each got one. I like mine better though. Hers is blue. I think gold is prettier." Everyone nodded their approval.

The children's plates were filled, and the adults sat down to eat. With the murmuring of the children in the background, the adults conversed about the present Christmas season and the volume of business in the Crane store. Shortly, however, the conversation was directed to the farm.

"It just doesn't seem like other Christmases when Laura was here," Betty, Ed's wife, observed.

"It's always a little gayer when she's around," John added.

"She didn't even come to church today. Can't understand that, missing church on a day like Christmas. Would have done her good," Helga critically observed. "Besides there are so many who would like to see her again. She hasn't been to church for a month now."

"Not since we went up on the hill to talk to Ray," John noted.

There was a momentary hush since everyone knew about Helga's big quarrel with Ray.

"Well, it's probably hard for her to get away right now with all those men to take care of you know," Betty concluded.

"Men?" Helga questioned, tearing some meat off of a drumstick between words, "two old cripples and a boy." She bit into a bone and cracked it. "I'll bet they're all starvin' up there today."

"I heard the sawmill sent up a ham for Christmas. They appreciate all the business he will soon be giving them," Ed explained.

Well that should make a pretty dinner," John replied. "Besides she's gotten to be a pretty good little cook. Both Ray and Gramp have said so."

"She's too good for that place. He's really been giving her the baloney; the way she's been hangin' on. I know she hates it now," Helga asserted.

"They've gone through a lot, and you can't hang it all on Ray. Bad luck is bad luck," John averred.

"He's the bad luck. Everybody's talking about him and his crazy ideas. Thinks he's going to make something of the Lennox name. And that old fool of a man is behind him. Next, the house'll be blown away," Helga ridiculed. "Addie was saying the whole block hates him now."

There was a scream from the side table and the smaller boy began to cry.

"What's the matter over there!" Ed yelled.

"He took some of my pie!"

The mother got up, lifted the older boy from his chair and pushed him toward the living room. "You go in and sit on the sofa. You're all done eating anyway," she scolded. The boy, wailing, ran into the living room where he continued sobbing and sucking his thumb.

"What did ya do that for?" Ed complained. "There's plenty of pie to go around."

"Sure we'll give him more pie if he wants it," Helga affirmed.

"Not now, later," Betty said.

"Anyway, like I was saying," Ed continued, "he's had enough support from us. You could probably offer him yer whole trucking outfit, and he'd still refuse it."

They ate in silence. As they were getting ready for after-dinner cocktails, the phone rang. Helga Crane wiped her mouth off and answered.

"Merry Christmas, Mother!" Laura greeted.

"Merry Christmas to you. We were just talking about you a moment ago and how we miss you this year."

"Oh we're having a great time up here."

"I bet," the mother spoke solemnly.

"We had a real nice ham. I've never seen Gramp so hungry and young acting."

"We're having a great time, too." In the background Helga heard a peal of men's laughter.

"You should see the ruby Gramp gave me. It's so beautiful. His wife used to—"

"It's probably an old imitation."

"I'll bring it along and show it to you, mom."

"When are you comin' down again?"

"Next weekend."

"Stop here next Sunday and we'll go ta church together. There's a few things I've got to tell you."

"O.K. but just wait, mom." Laura put Ray on the phone who responded with a "Merry Christmas!"

"Oh," Helga replied. There was a pause and Ray gave the receiver back to Laura.

After the conversation Helga returned to the table. "Well, she says that they're all havin' fun up there. That guy sure has her just where he wants her."

"The only one in the family and a spoiled brat," Ed contended.

"What spoiled brat, Daddy?" the little girl asked.

"I'm not a spoiled brat!" the little boy shouted, looking concerned at his sister.

"You two hush up now," the mother threatened.

"It's about time that we opened our presents now." Then Helga smiled, got up, and walked into the living room.

XX.

Ray decided to cut logs for the mill to process and sell. The family had exhausted most of its cash and now was dependent upon the trees for a living. Gramp offered to dig into his meager savings to help out, but Ray said that they would manage with the trees. The mill wanted high grade oak which would be cut for a furniture company in Lake City. Thus, the mill would select its own trees for cutting.

One morning at the beginning of January, Jim Sproule, co-owner of the lumber mill, drove into the yard in a company truck. Sproule, who was accustomed to bellowing orders at the employees of the mill, always conversed in a semi-shout. He was a husky man, a man used to wrestling with logs most of his life. In doing business, he drove a hard bargain. Although loud, he was a no-nonsense man whose speech was so laconic that the customer never knew for certain whether to attack or to defend. Only experienced businessmen dealt with him successfully.

At the kitchen table Ray and Sproule, with Gramp and Laura looking on, immediately went to work on a contract.

"Would you like to look at the woods first?" Ray suggested.

"I know all your woods!" Sproule shouted.

"There's about four acres of top grade oak left in Townline Woods, and I've got to have at least 13,000 dollars for it," Ray recommended.

"Sure!"

"I'd like 4,000 dollars in advance," Ray added.

"Why sure!" Sproule bellowed.

"That's a fair 'n' square deal," Gramp interjected.

"We know!"

"I'll sign right now under those terms," Ray maintained.

"I kin git six acres down the road for 12,000!" Sproule cried.

"Where?" Ray asked.

"Granger's woods!"

"His oak doesn't come near mine," Ray declared.

"Just about," Sproule concluded, as he put the contract back into his pocket. "I'll give you 12,000 for the acreage, 4,000 down, take it or leave it!" Sproule asserted.

There was silence. Ray looked at Gramp. "What do ya think, Gramp?"

"Wail," Gramp paused. "It still sounds O.K. I giss." Laura shook her head affirmatively as he spoke.

"Why sure!" Sproule roared. He placed the contract back on the table and read the simple terms to them. The mill was to get four specified acres of oak for 12,000 dollars with 4,000 in advance. The owner would do most of the labor with one man supplied by the mill three days a week. Ray and Sproule signed the contract with Gramp and Laura serving as witnesses.

As Sproule was about to leave, Ray suggested that he could use two men later on to help build the barn.

"Why sure! Why sure!" Sproule shouted, slamming the door as he left.

Gramp began doing what he called his share of the work. His hip, he claimed, felt almost like new, and he frequently went with Ray into the woods and worked until late afternoon. Ray had borrowed a powerful chain saw from Hibler. Each morning he would cut down several choice trees. Then he and Gramp, aided thrice weekly with an extra hand, would wedge the logs into quarters. Gramp enjoyed driving his wedge and watching the mighty oak logs split open.

The old man seemed oblivious to the disappearing trees. Each day he went out and swung his sledge at new logs. And with each load of logs, the woods receded. If Gramp felt bad about the decimation, he kept it to himself. Even when friends pointed out the growing ruins, he continued working, uncomplainingly. The only criticism he had was of himself, that he had lain around long enough and that it was time that he earned his keep. But the woods receded westward.

The resiliency of the old man was remarkable. He attempted to match Ray in desire and in fortitude. Even some of the villagers began talking about the tough old man among the oaks. And his determination grew. He got up at 8:00, then 7:00, and finally at 6:00. He even insisted upon making breakfast, "like in the good old days," but Laura politely shooed him out of the kitchen. Gramp began to brag about his health and vigor. He felt like a stud stallion at mating time, he told some of his old cronies in Landville one day when he rode down in a lumber truck. "Jist watch out fer me now," he began telling people.

Ray was satisfied with his source of revenue. They had enough money to last them until spring now. Then, when he had to buy more cattle, he would get another advance on another section of woods. When Gramp wondered where they would go after finishing Townline woods, Ray asserted that they would start on the southwest woods, where more high quality oak grew. Gramp remonstrated that with the end of the trees, life on the farm would end too.

"All them woods is where you grew up," Gramp reminded Ray.

"The woods mean nothin' to me now. It's jist another cash crop. Oak is in demand now, and I'm not goin' ta pass up the good prices."

"I wonder what yer folks'd say if they could see what we've done," Gramp looked west as he spoke. "Yer mother always enjoyed that woods so, 'n' liked ta listen ta the robins in the evening, 'n' watch the sun set through the boughs. This spring'll be sad with Townline woods all gone."

"I'll tell ya, Gramp, I'm not doin' this jist for me, ya know. You and Laura are part of this too. You need somethin' ta eat too," Ray responded.

"Wail, I was hopin' you'd spare a few of 'em."

"You'll always have the big oaks along the driveway. They'll always stand," Ray consoled.

Gramp resigned himself to cutting trees. "What's gotta be's gotta be, I giss," was his conclusion.

By the end of January, they had sawed beyond the rocky ridge where Ray, as a boy, used to fight imaginary Indians and capture imaginary bandits. Now covered by deep layers of snow and surrounded by huge snow-covered piles of branches, the ridge looked like a capsizing ship among awesome swells. Many of the oaks beyond the ridge were large and of excellent quality. On days when the employee from the mill did not work, Ray cut these large oaks, split them, and dragged them alongside the barn where later they would be cut into heavy beams for the new barn. Ray did not believe he was breaking the terms of the contract since he and Gramp, working long days, always had more wood cut than the trucks could handle.

Ray had decided to build what he called a storm-proof barn. The framework would be sturdier with more beams and supports. Gramp eyed certain trees and marked them for the barn. Later after they were halved or quartered, Hibler would bring his saw rig over and cut the beams.

Hibler had left the Lennox farm at the end of December to work with Steinhauser on a job in another county. They had agreed that, since Ray needed a quick income and could not afford to split the profit with Hibler, it would be best to call the mill in to finish the job. Later they might get together again to do some more work. Hibler promised that he would help with the barn later on.

A warm spell came in February, melting the snow and making the woods muddy and slippery. Work was slowed down by the adverse conditions. However, the high quality oak was in demand, and the mill was determined to keep production at an even keel. In addition to their man already in the woods, the mill asked for and received permission to put on another man. Ray agreed to the proposal, eager to get the remaining 8,000 dollars due when all the selected oak was cut.

The two experienced men came up every day and worked eight or nine hours struggling in the slush and grime. When the trees fell, branches snapped, rooting up the ground and sending slush and dirt in all directions. The woods was on a gradual hillside, and the men had to be especially careful when preparing to split the logs.

Adequate footing was a prerequisite for swinging the sledge hammers. Often the worker, believing he had solid footing, suddenly slipped as he raised his heavy hammer. Usually by noon the men's trousers were wet. But the four men worked on through February, adapting themselves to the changing conditions but nearing the completion of their work.

At the beginning of the operation the lumber trucks drove right into the woods and were loaded. However, as February wore on, it was determined that the heavily loaded trucks were beginning to sink too far in the thawing ground. A gap was made in the fence along Townline Road, and the truck backed up into the woods as far as it could. The men dragged the quartered logs the twenty to thirty feet down the hill and stacked them near the truck. Then a mechanical loader lifted them aboard. The process was slow. Only one large load of logs per day was hauled to the mill.

Not all the trees were cut, just the prime oak that the mill required. Smaller oaks, other species of trees, and bushes were left standing. However, when the oaks crashed to earth, they demolished everything in their path. Branches were ripped off smaller trees, wild berry bushes were flattened, and the habitat of wildlife ruined. One large oak fell accidentally into a grove of small pines which Gramp had planted three years before, completely destroying them. In the evening before leaving the woods, the men gathered the wreckage of branches from the day's work and threw them into a huge pile. They then tossed kerosene on and lit the pile. The conflagration each evening drew many spectators. Many villagers, out of habit, drove up prior to the blaze to witness the spectacle from start to finish. Some observed humorously that the brush fires were even more spectacular than Ray's barn fire.

From the living room window, Laura always watched the flames. In the darkness, she saw the silhouettes of the men coming, going, stooping, and rising as they gathered pieces of branches and limbs to throw on the fire. Sometimes the men would extend their arms and legs in warming gestures. Now and then one would toss a snowball into the flames and listen to the hiss. Always when the burning took place, she observed a solitary figure sitting on a log watching the holocaust. She knew his thoughts as he sat there watching.

Near the end of February, the men worked on the final acre of the woods. Huge, black volcanic-looking mounds of charred wood and ashes marred the hillside where the great trees had once stood. Heaps of snow and mud mixed with broken branches and chips of wood littered the ground along the areas where the huge trunks had fallen. Half-broken trees and shattered bushes hung limply as if in a daze. Here man was at work. The site of his labors told of a ferocious struggle. A war raged here, obliterating the land.

Each day at noon, Gramp and Ray went to the house to eat a quick lunch and change their clothes, usually wet from the waist down. One day when he was particularly soaked, Gramp limped noticeably as they entered the house. He had slipped and fallen over a log that morning, and his old nemesis, the left hip, bothered him again. In addition, he had developed a slight cold and frequently had to blow his nose. However, he insisted upon returning to the woods to finish up a tree he was working on. Laura and Ray were determined to keep him inside.

"You can help me around the house," Laura suggested. She had been busy since Christmas. Once a week she went to Landville to buy groceries and run other errands. She had begun baking now and discovered that it was a creative outlet for pent-up anxieties. And besides it brought much needed conversation to the kitchen table. Both Ray and Gramp always complimented her on her efforts, even when the dish was not a total success.

"I'll help ya with yer bakin' now," Gramp offered. "I ain't hardly done any cookin' or bakin' in two years now."

"It's Ray who needs you more than me," she answered.

"Yep, I'll be back out there tomorrah. I'm goin' ta drink a lot a root tea today," the old man responded. Root tea was a concoction made from herbs which were collected during the summer. It was an old recipe for cough medicine handed down through the generations. Gramp mixed liberal amounts of brandy with his medicine and said it was good.

"You'd better wait a few days and see how you feel. You can help me with the washing if you want to do something."

"I'll do the washin' fer ya, all the trousers. That must be a big chore anyhow."

Laura agreed that it would be a big help for her. She did not let the soiled overalls accumulate but washed them almost every day, even though there wasn't a full load in the machine. Ray frequently complained about the waste of electricity with such small wash loads. When Ray complained about the washing, Gramp offered to do the work by hand. He believed clothes lasted longer when kept out of machines. However, after being criticized for his old-fashioned ideas a number of times, he remained silent while the topic was broached.

"I'm gonna use that old wash tub like I did years ago. Bet I git the stuff jist as clean as you'd with that machine. But I'm only doin' the men's things, not ladies' clothes," Gramp asserted.

"Don't worry, I wouldn't think of mixing my clothes with all those dirty trousers," Laura chided.

"Wail, we ain't got germs. This is good, clean dirt up here on the hill." He chuckled at what he thought was a profound statement.

"You've got lots of germs right now, cold germs, and maybe you shouldn't be washing clothes even. Last time, you got as wet as the clothes you were washing."

"Wail, I'm gonna have me a stiff cup of root tea later on, 'n' you'll see an improvement. I feel fine now. Nose runs a little, 'n' throat's a little sore. That's all," he assured her.

"Next time I go to town I'm going to get some cough medicine. That's the best stuff I think for colds," Laura counseled.

"Pshaw! That stuff's all poison." He suddenly began to cough.

"Take care of yourself. Maybe I'd better do all the clothes yet today," Laura recommended.

Gramp persisted. That afternoon he washed the overalls and trousers and got wet as Laura had predicted would happen. Gramp merely changed and cleaned himself. Later in the day he made his famous root tea, mixed with strong brandy. After drinking the potion, he got tired and went to bed.

XXI.

The next day Gramp's cold had become worse. He coughed and blew his nose frequently. He complained about feeling a little dizzy and feverish. However, Gramp's problems were forgotten when, at noon, Ray announced that the Townline woods would be finished that evening and 8,000 dollars would be theirs. They were both elated. Ray got out his checkbook and calculated how much money they would have on hand to begin the new barn, and Laura planned a special dinner for that evening.

Early in the afternoon she drove to Landville and bought a beef roast, an assortment of fruits and vegetables, and the condiments she believed were necessary for a first-rate meal. Then she paid a short visit to her mother, as she frequently did on her weekly shopping trips.

"Soon now we'll begin the super barn. We've already got all the materials ready to go," Laura bragged.

"How are ya going ta pay all the super help?" Helga asked tauntingly.

"Oh, no problem. Granger will help. Hibler will help, and two of Ray's friends from town said that they might help in their spare time."

"You think they'll all work for nothing?"

"With the 8,000 dollars we're getting tonight, we'll have close to 10,000 on hand. Ray plans to start selling from the big woods in the back of the farm as soon as he can. We'll be able to pay our help," Laura asserted.

As Laura spoke, there was a squeaking sound, and the front door slowly opened. Then Addie Scrang's head slowly appeared.

"Hi," she called. "Just thought I'd stop 'n' say hi."

"Come in," Mrs. Crane invited.

Dylan, who was sitting in a corner of the living room awkwardly playing with blocks, looked up and shouted, "Wa, Wa, Wa," and then giggled. They all laughed.

"What a smart little boy," Addie observed. "He reminds me of my Jimmy when he was a half year old. Sharp as a tack he was. What else does he do?"

"Oh, not much. About all he does is crawl around and get into things," Laura replied.

"Well, my little Jimmy could stack blocks three or four high when he was six or seven months. But he was always a smart boy. How is it up on the farm? I hear the woods is nearly gone now. You'll be buildin' again, huh?"

"As I was telling Mom, we hope to begin right away, next week, weather permitting."

"Already!" Addie was surprised. "They say ya nearly starved this winter."

"Where did you hear that!" Laura said sharply.

"Oh, that's what they say," Addie insisted.

"Well, you'd better listen to them more carefully after this," Laura warned. "Well, I guess I'd better get home and get that roast in the oven. Ray said all the men, including Jim Sproule, will be eating with us tonight. We plan to have a grand time. Come Sweetie." She picked Dylan up. "When we get everything in order, we'll have you up again. I think you all will change your minds about Ray some day." The mother merely stared at her as she left the house with her son in her arms.

That evening, Ray, Sproule, and the men entered the kitchen in an atmosphere of tenseness. Ray, who was pale and glum-looking, went immediately to the writing desk in the living room and returned with the contract.

"I know about that," Sproule shouted, waving Ray away.

"It says right here that I'm ta git 12,000 dollars fer the four acres of oak with 4,000 down 'n' 8,000 at the completion of the job. Now I 'n' you both know that there was more than four acres. The little I kept out is not worth no thousand dollars."

"Ya get 7,000 dollars for the remaining oak. Take it or leave it," Sproule bellowed.

"What's this all about?" Laura questioned.

"He's goin' to give us only 7,000 final payment. Claims I kept out a thousand dollars' worth of wood to rebuild the barn," Ray spoke glumly.

"That's right. You broke the contract," Sproule clamored.

A delicious smell of roast beef filled the kitchen. The table was set with six places: napkins, silver, glasses, cups, and plates, all neatly arranged according to dining etiquette. Large candles burned on either end of the table where little Dylan sat, clumsily eating applesauce with his fingers.

"You're breakin' the terms of the contract," Ray shouted. "You signed and agreed to pay me the four thousand down payment and 8,000 more when four acres of oak was delivered."

Sproule pointed at the contract and yelled, "Look at part two on the second page!"

Ray turned to the second page, and near the bottom, where he had not bothered to read, he saw the words, "...

payment after all the timber from the acreage has been delivered to the buyer." He slowly folded the contract and put it back into the envelope.

"I can't see why you don't give me that wood. Gramp and me put all those long hours in working for you, and that wasn't called for in the contract."

"We don't do business that way!" Sproule exclaimed.

"You're not gettin' that lumber back. And I don't need your damned money. Get out of my house, you lousy crook!" Ray shouted.

Sproule straightened up and looked at Ray as if he were about to swing, "Don't you threaten me with those stupid remarks. We all know what you're like, you wife abuser!"

"What's this!" Laura demanded.

"It's all over town the way he's been treating you. Whenever you want that seven thousand, you come down to the mill and get it." With that, Sproule and his men walked out.

There was silence as the lumber trucks roared away. Laura stared across her luxurious table.

"We might as well sit 'n' eat," she spoke solemnly.

"I'm goin' out ta take inventory," he replied.

"Am I supposed to eat by myself?"

"Where's Gramp?"

"He's not feeling well. You might as well taste the roast. I've put so much time into this dinner."

"It's all too fancy for me. I'm not in the mood for celebration right now."

Laura looked at him angrily. "It's always your moods that the rest of us have to live by. Don't you think the rest of us have feelings?" She asserted herself loudly.

"Don't you shout at me. I jist don't feel like eatin' now."

Dylan suddenly began giggling, and they both looked at his applesauce besmeared face.

"Why don't you clean that kid up. He's got applesauce all over everything," Ray ordered.

"You need not tell me what ta do. I can handle my affairs. Evidently you can't handle yours."

"And what is that supposed ta mean?" he stared at her intently.

"Oh, nothing," she replied and started to remove the roast from the oven. Ray left the kitchen and headed for the barn.

XXII.

THE NEXT MORNING RAY and Laura ate breakfast silently. The baby, again in the high chair, babbled and giggled as Laura fed him oatmeal. Ray, hunched over his bowl of cereal, ate solemnly. His right arm listlessly pushed food toward his mouth. Usually, he ate breakfast in five minutes and dashed out. But this morning he was a long time at the table since there was nothing on the farm which required his immediate attention.

"So what are you going ta do now?" Laura broke the silence.

"Oh, I've got some ideas," he muttered. "I'm gonna see what Gramp thinks."

"I don't know when he's coming to breakfast. He felt terrible yesterday. After what happened last night, I just don't know what's happening anymore. So what's your idea?"

"I really don't know yet. I'll let ya know when the time comes. Besides, there's no need fer you ta worry about anything. I kin handle everything."

She glared at him and was ready to retaliate, but she remained silent as she watched the tired, hunched profile solemnly eating oatmeal. She observed the calloused fingers, the disheveled hair, the blue work-clothes, and brogans. Here was one who loved the soil. Here was a tough, honest man who would never admit to defeat.

"At least you ought to try and get the money the mill still owes us," Laura reminded.

He said nothing, and they finished eating in silence. Finishing his coffee, Ray got up and looked out the window toward Landville. It was a bright, sunny day, and the snow was melting already, causing a small stream of water to run down the driveway. On a bush next to the house sat a solitary robin, the first of the year. Spring, he hoped, would come early. There would be so much to do this spring. The farm must be put in order.

The familiar tap of a cane was heard as Gramp neared the kitchen.

"Finally," Laura said.

Gramp coughed hoarsely as he neared the kitchen. He stopped, blew his nose, and then opened the door.

"Good mornin'," he spoke roughly.

"How's it going this morning?" Laura queried.

"Oh, I feel great this mornin'. That medicine of mine always does the trick. Wail, how are ya, young man? What'd ya see out that window?"

"It's a nice day," came a reply.

"Yea, what ya say we tackle that barn today."

There was silence.

"I giss I'll cook me up a couple of eggs." He coughed again and pulled out a large, blue handkerchief and blew his nose.

"I'll get your breakfast for you," Laura asserted. "Have a seat and I'll pour you some coffee."

"That cold sounds bad this morning," Ray declared.

"Wail they always sound the worst in the mornin'. It's in my throat mainly, I giss. Had a little trouble breathin' last night."

"You'd better take it easy for a few days. You look a little pale this morning," Laura mentioned as she poured the old man some coffee.

"I'll have me some of that oatmeal. Is it still nice and hot?"

"Don't ya want eggs?"

"No, ma'am, just oatmeal."

Before Gramp had a chance to eat some of the steaming food, his chest heaved mightily and he coughed profusely. Turning his head aside he coughed phlegm into his handkerchief. Soon the old man was busy eating.

Ray took a seat and drank some more coffee, absorbed in thought.

"Wail, I s'pose the boys from the mill are all done 'n' gone. Haven't heard no more noise from back of the house. Shore looks barren from out my bedroom winda. It's gonna seem strange with that woods gone. All the wildlife'll hafta move further down the road."

"Oh, I don't know about that, Gramp. I just saw a robin next to the window there. Maybe they'll come closer to the house now," Laura said.

"A robin, eh? Spring's closer than I thought. Oh, I'll be glad ta git out in the frish spring air again and smell the new turned sod. Spring's always bin excitin' here on the hill. When're we startin' on the barn?" Gramp looked sharply at Ray as he spoke.

"He refused to pay me the full eight thousand he owes me," Ray looked down at the table as he spoke.

"Refused? Why I've never knowed Jim Sproule to refuse payin' up. Loud-mouthed, but always pays up. What'd he say?"

"Claims the timber I kept back ta finish the barn is worth a thousand. Says I broke the terms of the contract. He won't pay up now."

"He offered us only seven thousand, and there is no way around it," Laura explained.

"Wail, I'll go down 'n' have a talk with that young man. He doesn't 'preciate what all we done for 'im this winter. He'll listen ta me."

"It won't do no good. Ya know how stubborn he can git," Ray pointed out.

"Wail, watcha plan ta do now? Give the wood back to 'im?"

"No, I'm gonna continue," Ray vowed. "I'm gonna call Hibler 'n' see if he'll saw all the beams for us. We kin work out by the day to repay him. Once everything is cut it'll take only a few of us ta do the building."

"That heavy-duty barn ya want'll take some doin'. It takes a lot of men ta hoist some of those big beams." Gramp's last words were heaved out by another gigantic cough which convulsed his frame. He coughed more phlegm into his handkerchief and then took a drink of coffee.

"Gramp, that cold is getting worse. You'd better not talk about building barns yet. What you need is plenty of rest," Laura suggested.

"Psah, there's plenty of rest in the grave. I plan ta be out gettin' plenty of frish air soon. That'll be the best—frish air. Anyway, as I was sayin', ya can't trust nobody no more. Why, I've known Jim since he was a kid. I don't understand. Won't pay up ya say?"

"Owes me eight thousand yet," Ray repeated. "From now on I'm taking all my business to the mill in Lake City."

"I think that's only a pulp mill in Lake City," Gramp reminded.

"Well, I'll find some place ta take it. I'll borrow one of John's big trucks and sell it ta some dealer somewhere," Ray offered.

"Where we gonna cut wood next?" Gramp asked.

"I'm goin' into the southwest forty as soon as the weather warms up so we kin git the tractor across the marshy area," Ray replied. "I'll ask Hibler to help us. There's some money in that woods."

"Hope you don't take any of those pine up on the hill," Gramp pleaded.

"No, jist the oak."

"What do you expect us to live on until then?" Laura asked. "That thousand you put in the checking account is getting sort of low. When I go shopping tomorrow, I'll stop by the mill and pick up all that money that he owes us. Maybe I can even talk him into giving us all he owes us."

"No, you won't!" Ray stormed. "I'll go 'n' get that money when I'm good 'n' ready for it. We've got plenty ta live on yet."

"Don't you folks worry. If ya need money, I've got plenty ta help ya out. Whenever ya need some, you jist let me know," Gramp offered.

"It's silly to let him keep money which is rightfully ours," Laura continued.

"Don't you call what I do silly," Ray warned, his face growing red. "I'm the boss here, and I decide what ta do. My plan is ta work fer Hibler for awhile 'til the weather improves. I'm gonna call 'im this morning 'n' see what he says about the southwest woods. Ya don't have ta worry;

we'll always have an income. There's always plenty of work around in the woods."

Gramp coughed hoarsely. This time he had to hunch over, holding his hands against his chest. The baby, who had been playing with beads attached to the side of the highchair, accidentally knocked over his bowl of oatmeal. Oatmeal splashed down the table leg, and the bowl rolled under the table. The child then slid down into the highchair and smiled jovially.

Ray picked up the bowl and placed it on the table. He glared at the child who smiled up at him. Then he grabbed Dylan roughly and set him up in the highchair. The tiny boy flailed his arms in protest and began to cry.

"Be quiet," Ray snapped. He grabbed a towel and briskly wiped the child's face.

"Yer gonna learn some manners around here," he spoke curtly, and Dylan wailed harder.

"And you've got to learn some manners too," Laura glared at her husband and then picked up the crying child and hugged him. "That's O.K., sweetheart. Mommy's got you now; you're safe. Hush. He picks on only little boys."

"I won't tolerate very much more of this foolishness. You're training 'im ta be jist like those spoiled brats of your uncle's."

Laura, paying no attention, walked quickly into the living room and closed the door.

"That boy wasn't doin' anything all that bad that ya had ta git so mean with 'im," Gramp reproved.

"She's always giving 'im her attention. Look at all the oatmeal on the floor. She feeds 'im as if he was a man. Eats only half of it, 'n' then she complains we don't have enough money. She wastes too much."

"Oh, I wouldn't say that. She's pretty careful most o' the time as I see it."

"She's gonna spoil 'im and he won't be worth a damn. It won't hurt if he's disciplined a little bit now and then. I don't believe he's ever been spanked."

"Wail, I believe I'll start cleanin' up these breakfast things a little," Gramp started to get up.

"No! Leave that fer her ta do."

"Whatever you say. Watcha gonna do now?"

"I'm gonna call Hibler 'n' see if he's got some work for us. I haven't seen 'im around for awhile."

"Told me once that he had a job somewhere up near Squaw Creek in Stone County."

Luckily, Ray reached Hibler on the phone that morning just before he and his crew left for work. They drove 35 miles north each day to the Squaw Creek National Forest where Hibler had a government contract to harvest oak. It was a very profitable deal, Hibler pointed out to Ray. He also told Ray that it would be a month or so before he could cut the beams. But Ray and Gramp were to come right away since there was plenty of work for everyone.

"Gramp, you'd better wait 'til your chest cold gets better," Ray suggested.

"Wail, giss I'll wait another day or so then. It's settled in my chest again, 'n' those are always bad ones."

While Gramp was talking, Ray was hurriedly putting on his coat.

"I'll see ya this evening, Gramp. So long."

When Ray had driven out of the driveway, Laura returned to the kitchen.

"Where did he go?"

"We're startin' work at Hibler's over by Squaw Creek; I'll be helpin' out in a day or so."

"How am I supposed ta get the shopping done when he takes the car?"

"Giss he never thought of that but—" Before Gramp could continue, he doubled over in a coughing spell. Then he sat down, exhausted, on the wall bench.

"Whew, that made me dizzy. I'm gonna make me some root tea and then rest a little bit."

"That's a good idea. Squaw Creek is a long ways. I'll never get to town anymore."

"Don't worry about gettin' ta town. Ya kin use my car whenever ya want to. Do ya need some money, too?" Gramp offered.

"No thanks. He's sure driving a long ways to work. It must be close to forty miles up there. That means he'll be home late again. How long is he working for Hibler?"

"Oh, we'll be workin' fer 'im maybe a month or two," Gramp asserted. He looked pale as he sat slumped over on the bench.

"I just don't know what's gonna happen now. I wish we'd give it all up and move to town. We've been scraping by ever since we moved up here. I know he's planning to buy cattle with what's left in the bank. He doesn't think about spending on his family."

"There'll be plenty of money now with me and him workin'. You needn't worry."

"That's not the only thing. All he thinks about is work and more work. He's gone from early in the morning until late at night. Around Christmas it wasn't so bad, but now it's worse than ever. Dylan and me don't exist anymore. We might as well not even be here. I wonder if he'd miss us if we left? I'm beginning to have doubts about it all."

Gramp coughed again, his eyes watering. His breathing came heavily. Finally he spoke, "He's over anxious now with the trick Sproule played on 'im. Ya kin hardly blame 'im. I'm goin' to town soon 'n' have a talk with 'im. He knows us Lennoxes well enough. We don't cheat."

"I guess Sproule wasn't fair, but Ray wasn't either. Maybe someday he'll learn how to get along with people," Laura observed.

The next morning after Ray had gone to work, Laura got herself and Dylan ready to go shopping. Excited, she hurried through breakfast, hardly thinking about Gramp who, although it was after nine o'clock, had not come for breakfast. She was intent with the idea of stopping at the sawmill to get all that money which Sproule owed them. She would deposit the money in the checking account and surprise Ray that evening with her initiative. Perhaps she might even convince Sproule to give them all the money he owed them.

Opening the writing desk, she discovered that the checkbook was gone. She couldn't believe it! He had now decided to deprive them of the money needed to buy groceries. Angered, she left the house, Dylan in arms, eager now to get the money from Sproule. She would teach him a lesson about pulling tricks. She even entertained the idea of keeping the money for herself.

Gramp had left his car keys on the table, and she thought of him again. He had taken a strong dose of root tea last night and, no doubt, slept extra well. She would not disturb him. Then her thoughts turned again to the missing checkbook and all the money that she would have soon. She drove mechanically to town, thinking.

At the mill she asked for Sproule. He received her cordially in his office and asked about the situation on the hill.

"Well, he's working for Hibler again over in Stone County."

"I'll say this much for him. He certainly likes to work," Sproule said emphatically.

"Yes, he likes to work. That's all he does, but we never seem to have much to show for it. I came down to do some shopping, but I don't even have a checkbook anymore."

"So he wants to deprive you of food, too. Your credit is good all over town. You don't have ta worry about that," Sproule stormed.

There was a pause.

"I've come after all the money you owe us."

"Oh, I gave that to your mother just this morning. You'll have to see her about it. I thought you probably knew by now."

"Cash!"

"No, a company check. It's the same thing. I told her to put it in an account for you. I see now that it is the wise thing to do."

"Oh, I see. I'll be able to do some grocery shopping after all today."

"If you did the smart thing you'd never have to worry about where the groceries are comin' from. I hear it's awfully rough up there for you and the little boy."

"Oh, sometimes, but money is our main problem right now. As soon as he gets the barn built, he's going to spend all the money we get to buy a herd of cattle," Laura pointed out. "He thinks I don't know how to handle money."

"If you never have any, I don't know how you can mishandle it."

"He thinks he knows what's best for us," Laura explained.

"Well, he has yet to prove that. If he knew what was best for you he'd sell that place. No one has ever made a profit up there. But don't you worry. The whole town is behind you. Just call on us if you need help!" Sproule exclaimed.

"I was wondering if you would pay us all that you owe us. After all, they helped you, and their labor must be worth something."

Sproule stared at her as if he couldn't believe what he was hearing. Then he protested vehemently, "I'll never give you any money that he'll waste trying to fix up that old place!"

"But a thousand was a lot to hold back," she murmured, "when we need it so bad."

"He did the holding back. He held back the best lumber, at least a thousand dollars' worth. No one breaks a contract with me!" he roared.

"You owe us a little more," she spoke softly.

"I owe you nothing!" came a shout.

"Well I thought maybe just a little," she insisted.

"I do things fair and square here. You go home now and get that money from your mother."

"All right. I'll see you." Laura said goodbye and drove to her mother's house. Helga Crane, who had been waiting, opened the door for her.

"Just tried to call you and got no answer. Say, I've really got a nice surprise for you. Jim Sproule brought a seven-thousand dollar check for you this morning. He said for you to open a checking account with it."

"I know. I just came from his place, and we talked about it," Laura affirmed.

"He's got a good idea. Open your own account, and you'll always have money for food."

"I'll have to think about that."

"Don't you worry. You've got all of us behind you," Helga declared.

"I can't even put money in the bank because he took the checkbook this morning." She gave her mother an ironic smile.

"What will he do next? Now he doesn't even want ya to have the checkbook. He thinks everything is his. Open your own checking account and show him something."

"I just don't know. He wouldn't be very happy if I did that, and I'm the one who has to live with him. I probably should give it to him."

"If he wants it, let him come and get it. Where is he?"

"Over in Squaw Creek working for Hibler again."

"I thought he was so interested in trying ta build that barn again."

"Well, we've got to have some money to live on," Laura asserted.

"You think that's what he's working for? He'll throw it all away on that farm again. Where's all that other money that Jim paid you?"

"Most of it's still in the bank. He plans to build the barn and buy cattle with it."

"He's not interested in you and the boy. It's about time you had your share of the earnings. Take this check and open your own account." She held out the check with one hand and pounded an end table with the other while she spoke.

Laura remained silent for awhile and stared at the check as it lay in her mother's lap.

"Well, I guess maybe I'd better take the check and give it to him," she reached for the check as she spoke.

"No!" her mother shouted. "I'll take it and open an account for you then, if you're so afraid of him. That'll teach him a lesson. What does he think you're supposed to buy food with?"

"I don't need money. Mr. Sproule just told me my credit's good all over town."

"Your credit is good for you and Dylan, not for him. Nobody'll give him anything. Trying to rebuild and rebuild, one failure after another and after the offers he's had here in town. No, he gets no more cooperation from us. With a wife and a kid to support you'd think he'd know better."

"Well, he is a hard worker and he has been trying," Laura contested.

"Trying doesn't count. It's results that count. Almost two years up there and still no results. I'm tired of arguing about it. I'll give you some money and you can get your shopping done. I'll take care of the check for you."

XXIII.

WHEN LAURA GOT HOME from shopping, after eleven o'clock, she was surprised that Gramp was not up. She put the grocery items away and decided to wait for awhile. The old man was very tired yesterday and with his bad cold, he required much sleep, she thought. Twelve o'clock came and still no sign of the old man. However, Laura's thoughts were not primarily concerned with Gramp's ailing condition. They were directed toward her predicament on the farm. She knew there would be a nasty scene that night when she told Ray about the money. She had best tell him and not let him find out by himself. But she reassured herself that she had done nothing wrong, that she had done nothing to bring on the problem. Then she thought of life on the hill the past two and a half years. She wondered if it had been a wasted life. She thought of her friends who had gone on to college or who had gone directly to work and were still single. Many had moved to the large cities. What was life like in a city? She thought of the lights, the glamour, and the excitement they must be enjoying. Was she sacrificing the best days of her youth up here on this lonely hill? She wondered. One o'clock came and still no sign of Gramp. She decided to investigate.

Upon entering his bedroom, she heard a wheezing as the old man labored to breathe. "Where have ya bin?" he asked weakly. "I called but no one's bin here all morning."

"I'm sorry, Gramp, but I've been shopping. I go every Friday morning, you know. I did not realize that you were so sick that you'd need me."

"Can't git up. Tried but fell back on the bed again. Got so dizzy." He spoke as if in a daze. "Leave me rest awhile. I'll be all right."

"I'd better call Doc Jones. You look awfully sick."

The old man didn't respond, but the wheezing continued.

"That cold is in your chest, Gramp, and that's a dangerous place to get one. We've got to get the doctor here to help you."

"What does he know. Jist leave me be. I'll be all right soon. I've had chest colds before."

Laura sensed that drastic action would have to be taken. She looked closely at the face that she had known all her life. Beads of perspiration now covered the face and ran down the cheeks into the white stubble of a three-day beard. His eyes, red and moist, stared out the west window where once the tall oak woods stood. With a light blanket covering his body, he lay as if in anticipation.

As Laura thought about the old man's plight and the course of action she would have to take, the phone rang and she left the old man's side to answer. It was her mother.

"We've gone ahead and put the money in a checking account for you. You'll have to come down and sign some papers from the bank."

"I wish you wouldn't have done that, Mom."

"Never mind. Sproule is giving you three hundred dollars extra. So don't get stubborn. The bank wants you to sign some papers I've got here. When can you do it?"

"I can't come now. Gramp's awfully sick, and I believe I'm going to have to call the doctor."

"You've got to sign before Ray hears about it, or you know what'll happen. That old man can take care of himself. He always has," Mrs. Crane persisted.

"He can hardly breathe, and I'm going to stay and help him."

"Don't worry about him. He's old and we're not responsible for him. Besides he's on their side."

"Well, I'm not leaving him. I need more time to think the whole thing over before I sign anything. If I decide to sign, I'll be down in the morning."

"Have it your way then," Helga spoke angrily. "But don't say anything to him about it." The conversation ended abruptly.

When Laura called the doctor's office, she was told that Doctor Jones was out visiting a patient. She then called the home of the visitation and was told that the doctor had gone home to take his afternoon nap, but would be back later. Determined, she called the old physician's house. The old man had a difficult time trying to understand her.

"Laura, oh you mean Mrs. Crane's daughter. What's your problem?"

"It's Gramp. He's got a terrible cold."

"I can't do much fer 'im. Put 'im to bed and make sure he gets plenty of rest."

"He's got a bad fever and can hardly breathe."

"Can't eat? Lot of hot liquids and plenty of rest. That's the ticket fer a cold. Those Lennoxes are a tough brood. Don't worry about old Grandpa Lennox."

Laura felt helpless. How could she make the old doctor understand?

"Come up and see him, please. He is very bad. Please come up right away."

"Well, I was about ta take my nap. Maybe after supper—a cold is nothing to worry about. He gets them every year."

"But he can't even stand without getting dizzy."

"Symptoms of a bad cold. Head's all stuffed up. Don't worry. I've got to run now. I'm treating a patient. Mrs. McGerty's fallen again. This time she sprained an ankle. There's bad swelling. It's a serious case. I'm gettin' back to her after my nap. See ya after supper. Bye now."

"But..." Laura attempted to protest, but the doctor hung up.

Laura returned to the bedroom where Gramp still lay in deep perspiration, the fever having not abated. The asthmatic breathing continued.

"Doc is coming right after supper. He'll help you." She tried to speak cheerfully.

"Don't need no help from that old man. Jist leave me be. I think I'm feelin' a little better already."

"Well, he's coming up to look at you," Laura repeated.

Gramp said nothing.

Laura wiped the old man's forehead again and asked him if he would like some soup. He assented, and she went to the kitchen to prepare it. Her thoughts turned to the money and the decision she must make. She longed to have her own spending money to buy nice things which other women had. But her husband would never allow her a personal account. She decided against the idea in order to maintain some harmony within the family. She decided, however, to keep the extra three hundred dollars for herself. She would keep it at her mother's house to use in case of emergencies.

When she got back to Gramp with the soup, he had covers piled over him and was shivering.

"What's happened now? Are you cold?"

"Suddenly I'm shiverin'," he replied weakly.

"Well, here's some nice hot soup for you."

The old man drank his soup, coughing in the middle of the meal.

It was after seven when Doc Jones drove into the farmyard. By this time Gramp was sweating again. The old doctor carefully studied his patient, cocking his head a little bit to one side.

"Yer kinda rough lookin', young man," the doctor pronounced.

"'n' that's how I feel. This cold has settled in my chest, 'n' I kin hardly breathe at times."

"Well, let me take a look." The doctor began by carefully listening to Gramp's breathing through his stethoscope. Then he checked eyes, nose, throat, and pulse. Soon he was listening to the breathing again, asking Gramp to breathe deeply. Finally, the doctor made his diagnosis.

"My friend, you've got yourself a good case of pneumonia. One lung sounds pretty bad and the other's got a touch. The best place for you is the hospital over in Lake City."

"I ain't goin' ta no hospital. I ain't that bad."

"Whatever you say. Serious cases need oxygen. If it hits that other lung you'll be in bad shape. But with plenty of rest and medication, let's see what we can do. I'll make out a prescription fer penicillin and give you something to help you sleep tonight. Then we'll hope for the best."

"I ain't goin' in no hospital," Gramp continued to argue.

"Gramp, pneumonia is something serious. You should take the doctor's advice," Laura pleaded.

The doctor again listened to Gramp's breathing, shaking his head as he listened.

"How long has it been this way?"

"Today's been the worst," Gramp replied.

"Well, we'll get ya somethin' ta stop that infection." The doctor then packed up his things and made out a prescription. "Take this to town and get it filled." He gave the prescription to Laura and left.

"I'm going down town and see if I can get this taken care of before the drugstore closes. They're open late on Fridays, aren't they?"

"Yes, 'til nine or ten on Friday," the doctor replied.

Having no money, Laura decided to go to her mother's place first and borrow from the extra three hundred that was being held for her. She got Dylan ready for the second time that day. When she was ready to leave the house, Ray drove in from his long day at work. He was tired and came into the kitchen expecting to find food in some stage of preparation for him.

"Where are you going this time of night?" he snapped.

"Gramp is sick with pneumonia and I have a prescription to fill," she held up the piece of paper.

"Where did you get that from?"

"The doctor just left. Gramp is very sick," she asserted.

"Doc Jones?"

"Yes, I don't have any money to buy medicine. Give me the checkbook."

"I'll keep the checkbook," he shot back.

Laura, angered but in no mood to argue, walked past him, with child in arms, and out the door.

"How are you goin' ta pay for it?" Ray demanded.

"Don't worry. I've got lots of relatives." She was not about to tell him about her windfall. As long as he remained cruel and inconsiderate, she would never cooperate.

"Jist wait a minute!" Ray yelled. "Come back in for a minute."

She re-entered the house as Ray disappeared into the living room. She sat on the wall bench with Dylan on her lap. Shortly, Ray returned with a twenty dollar bill in his hand.

"I didn't think he was that bad," he said as he handed her the money. "'n' bring all the change back to me," he requested.

"Can I have the car keys? I don't like to drive Gramp's old car."

"It's nearly out of gas and I don't have enough money ta put some in. I'm goin' to the bank first thing in the morning," he offered.

"O.K." She lifted Dylan and opened the door.

"You kin leave Dylan here with me; it'll be easier for you," Ray suggested.

"No!" she insisted and left the house.

She went directly to the drugstore and discovered that it was closed. The sign on the door said, "9-8 Friday." She decided to go to her mother's house to call Burt Feir, owner of the store, since this was an emergency.

Her mother was surprised to see her so soon. "I didn't expect you here tonight already. How did you get away without him knowing about it?"

"I've come to call Mr. Feir. I've got to get some medicine for Gramp."

"These bank papers'll take only a minute to sign. Everything is ready." Helga pointed to some papers lying on the coffee table.

"I'm calling Mr. Feir first. Gramp's got pneumonia and needs medicine bad." She headed for the phone.

"Why are you so concerned about them? They aren't concerned about you. Take care of your own business first."

Laura ignored her mother and proceeded with her phone call. A babysitter answered and explained that the Feirs had gone to a concert in Lake City and wouldn't be home until quite late.

"I've got to get that medicine," Laura insisted. "Maybe the doctor can get it for me." As she looked up the doctor's number, her mother laid the papers down next to her.

"Don't worry about the medicine. That can wait 'til tomorrow. What you should be worried about is where you'll get money from. Do you have money to buy the medicine?"

"Yes, but I also planned to borrow from that extra three hundred dollars he gave you."

"Well, that's going in the account with the rest of the money where it will be safe. If you sign these papers, you'll have your own account. What are you waiting for anyway?" She handed a pen to Laura.

Laura thought for awhile and then signed the papers without realizing the import of her actions, since her immediate attention was on filling the prescription for Gramp.

She called Doc Jones, who told her she could wait 'til morning. But he also suggested she might find a drugstore open if she drove to Lake City. Laura insisted that the doctor come and open the store for her. But the doctor balked, saying he was in his night clothes and nearly in bed. Besides, he argued, old Gramp Lennox was tough and there would be no problem. The conversation ended abruptly. And Laura, discouraged, thought about driving to Lake City.

"I might just drive to Lake City and get the medicine. Doc says there are drugstores open there."

"In that old car? It's not safe. Besides it's probably out of gas, and I know you don't have any money."

Laura remained silent.

"Why don't you two stay here overnight and go to the drugstore in the morning?"

"No! I can't let Gramp alone the way he is," Laura insisted. "He's pretty bad today."

"Can't let Gramp alone!" the mother mocked. "His grandson is the one who should be taking care of him. Where is he tonight?"

"He put in a long day, and I did too. I guess I'd better be going," Laura asserted.

"Without his medicine?" the mother chided.

"We'll have to wait 'til tomorrow." Laura picked up the sleeping child and drove home.

Ray was already upstairs preparing for bed. Laura went directly to the old man's room and heard the wheezing well before she got there.

"Gramp, didn't you take the medicine Doc left to help you sleep?"

Gramp stared up at her. In the artificial light his face appeared wan and shrunken. His physique seemed smaller. It all looked so unnatural to her as she gazed down upon the sick man whom she had admired for so long. She felt helpless, as instinctively, she tried to think of something to do to ease the old man's suffering.

"Gramp, why didn't you take your sleep medication?"

"That stuff doesn't help any," he spoke feebly.

"The drugstore was closed, and I couldn't get the other medication, but I'll get it first thing in the morning.

The old man was silent.

"Don't worry, Gramp, we'll have you up soon," Laura consoled.

He stared at her intently and then spoke as if he had just remembered something. "I wish you'd make me some root tea so I kin sleep some tonight." He gasped for breath. "It's always hilped me."

Laura, not willing to argue, conceded to the old man's request. He told her how to mix the tea and ordered a rather strong concoction. She promptly made it for him. After consuming the hot liquid, Gramp declared that he felt better already.

"You'd better take this medicine too," Laura insisted. She got a glass of water and put two pills on a chair next to him. "I'm going to sleep on the sofa in the living room tonight. Don't be afraid to call if you need something." She left the door to his bedroom ajar. If he became worse, she would call an ambulance from Lake City, no matter how much he protested. However, the old man slept reasonably well that evening.

The next morning, as Ray and Laura ate breakfast, they discussed the problem created by the old man's illness.

"I don't think he's sick enough to be put in a hospital, if Doc didn't say so," Ray contended.

"He's never been this way before. He doesn't eat, can't get up, and has difficulty breathing. I think we ought to do something soon before it's too late," Laura argued.

Ray pondered the implication of her words. "Well let's get the medicine and let him take it for a few days and then see what happens. He might as well be here as in the hospital."

Shortly Laura, Ray, and child drove together to town. Since they would be back in a half hour, they decided it was safe to leave Gramp alone. They parked on Main Street, and he went to the bank and she to the drugstore. When they met back at the car, he asked her if she needed money for grocery shopping.

"No, when I need to shop, I'll just take the checkbook," she answered confidently.

"I think it would be best if I keep the checkbook for awhile. We're a little tight with money 'n' we must be careful."

"You're making money now working every day. I don't see why I can't have a little money when I need it."

"The way I have it planned, we'll be back on our feet soon, if we're careful. Once things are flourishin' everyone'll have confidence again. This time nothing'll take that barn down. It will be a solid one but will cost quite a bit more. So we've got ta conserve now. I'll give ya some money each week ta buy the things ya want. So don't worry." As he spoke he handed her a twenty dollar bill.

He stopped and filled up with gas, and then they headed for the hill. "I hope this old crate holds together fer a couple more months while I'm drivin' so far ta work," he complained. He headed west along Townline Road and then suddenly turned left across the bridge to the sawmill. Laura was startled.

"We have ta get home to see how Gramp is and give him his medicine," she reminded.

"I'm jist goin' ta tell him ta mail that check he owes me before he forgets. It'll only take a minute."

Laura became frightened and decided to tell him everything before he learned it from Sproule. "The money's already in the bank."

"Huh? Who are you kiddin'?"

"He gave it to Mother and she put it in the bank," Laura confessed.

He stopped the car quickly, befuddled. "Your mother did what?" he spoke incredulously.

"They insisted that it be put in the bank and that's where it is."

"What bank? In what account?" he demanded loudly.

"In our account," she hugged the child tightly and prepared for the worst.

"It is not in our account. It wasn't this morning. Where is that money?" he shouted.

The child, who had been peacefully resting, opened his eyes, looked fearfully at his father, and began to cry.

"They all insisted that it be put in my name," she answered.

"Your name? What in hell is your name! We're gettin' back to that bank!" he yelled.

Dylan broke into a loud wail as Ray recklessly wheeled the car around, throwing the mother and child against the right door. Laura hit her head against the window, and the baby screamed louder. Ray, oblivious to all, drove quickly downtown. He rushed into the bank and went immediately to Mr. Behof, head teller and president of the Landville State Bank.

"All right, where's the illegal account in my wife's name?" he demanded.

"We have an account in her name, and don't you call it illegal. Everything in this bank is legal," Mr. Behof responded angrily.

"Here, put it all in my account." He put his checkbook on the table in front of Behof.

"Your wife will have to sign an agreement to release the money," Behof explained.

"All I want ta do is make a deposit of two thousand dollars that's already my money. That other account cannot be legal."

"I'm sorry. Mrs. Crane brought the papers over this morning, signed into account by Laura. If you want to change accounts, she'll have to agree to it," Behof added.

"Mrs. Crane! She's behind this whole thing." Now bitterness was added to his anger. He would show them presently who was boss. He returned to the car to get Laura. She and the child were gone. He knew where to find her and drove toward Helga Crane's house. As he approached the house, he saw a shiny red sports car back out of the driveway and roar away. Everett Ernst did not look at him nor acknowledge his presence. Ray, now seething, entered the house quickly.

Laura was seated on the living room sofa crying softly. Dylan, now in familiar confines, had stopped crying and was playing with tassels on a pillow. When Ray stormed in the child quickly climbed upon his mother's lap. Ray and Helga confronted each other.

"My daughter has had enough of you. You are not fit to live with."

Ray ignored the reproach and spoke to Laura, "C'on we're goin' home."

"That is not a home," Helga responded.

"Oh yeah, and who are you, ya big thief! Taking my money 'n' doin' what ya please with it," Ray glared at her furiously, as if ready to strike.

"Sproule brought the money to her. She deserves something after all the hardships she's had up there with you," Helga countered.

"I don't care who brought it. Yer a big troublemaker. Always have been. I know why that husband of yers died so young. You harassed 'im ta death. And don't start on me or I'll put you in yer place," he clenched his fists. "Are ya comin'? Or is Ernst takin' you home?"

Laura continued sobbing. "Let me rest awhile. I'm so tired. Just let me be. I'll go back later."

Helga said nothing.

Ray continued to look at Laura. Then he quickly turned and left.

Laura, lost in thought, forgot momentarily all about Gramp. She knew the money in her account was not hers rightfully to keep. But as long as he treated her as if she could not be trusted with their checkbook, she would keep the money.

It was going on eleven when the young woman finally realized what time it was and decided she had better find a way up to the farm. However, her mother suggested that Ray probably went home to look after the old man.

"Besides," she advised, "it's his business to take care of his relatives."

"I know he went right to work, and poor Gramp's there all alone. I've just got to get up there and get the medicine to him," she entreated. "I'll even walk back if I have to."

"He went right to work, and you can stay right here."

Laura got up. "Well, I can't let him alone up there. He could even be dying. I'll leave Dylan with you."

"Jist wait a moment," the mother insisted. "John'll be stopping by for lunch soon. He can take you up, if you think it's your duty to go."

Laura reluctantly agreed to the idea. However it was after twelve before John arrived. Meanwhile Laura had called the farm to see if by chance Ray had stopped there. The phone rang and rang, and there was no response.

"I hear you and yours had a little squabble over money," John teased as he drank coffee. "I think he's tryin' to make too much out of that old place." As her mother and Uncle John discussed and debated the problem and how to resolve it, Laura worried.

She dreaded that the worst had happened. Maybe she should call Doc Jones, and they could ride up together. Maybe she should call an ambulance now, just in case.... Gramp was an old man, and he must not be left alone another moment.

"I don't know how he plans to build that barn again. I guess he intends to make something out of all that wreckage that's layin' around up there. No one in town plans to help him this time because they all think he's so foolish," John explained.

"He's had his chances but is too silly to know what's good for him," Helga agreed. "It's his mess and his life. Let him go ahead by himself and we'll see what happens. But I wish he'd leave others alone."

Laura suddenly got up. "I've got to go. I'm not going to leave him up there alone with pneumonia."

"Pneumonia!" John was surprised. "A tough old codger like him? Why, he has always taken care of himself."

"That's what I say," Mrs. Crane concurred.

"How long has he been sick?" John asked.

"Bad for just a few days. But he can't get out of bed, and I've got to get back to feed 'im and give him his medicine."

"Well, if you're that worried, we'll—"

"Just finish eating first. No one else seems to be that worried about him," Mrs. Crane growled.

"I'm just about done anyway," he spoke, getting up from the table. It was obvious that the girl was very distressed. "Get your things and we'll go."

It was nearly one o'clock and John was anxious to be on his way. He had a large load of livestock to haul to Lake City yet that day and was bound westward for his first pickup. Laura grew apprehensive as the truck approached the farm.

"Say hello to old man Lennox for me," John requested. "I'd stop by, but I'm in sort of a hurry."

He left the mother and child off at the driveway entrance and roared on. Laura rushed toward the house eager to administer the medicine which the old man should have received hours ago.

She heard gasping as she approached the old man's bedroom, and her heart began to pound. Then she gazed upon a pathetic figure laboring for life. Gramp's face and hands had turned bluish, and his eyes, sunken and blank, stared out the window, as if fixed upon something in the distance. Frequently he shuddered as he lay with no blankets covering his body. He looked like someone who was in the process of drowning. She pulled the blankets up over the heaving chest. He blinked his eyes but the fixed stare continued.

"Gramp! Gramp! What's happened?" she tried to make him understand. His eyes fell upon her momentarily. "Gramp, can you understand me?" Again the eyes moved from her to the window, where now a flock of returning birds were winging west over the remains of the decimated woods.

"Gramp, what's the matter?" she spoke helplessly. Again his eyes focused upon her momentarily and then returned to the window, as if in expectation.

"I'm all alone now; they're all gone," came a scarcely audible voice. "They've all left me now."

"I'm here. You're not alone anymore, Gramp," she tried to comfort him. She placed her hands on his shoulders. "Do you understand me?"

The old man said nothing but resumed the blank stare out beyond her. His white hair was disheveled, and she felt like combing it. His gasps came harder as if air were a fleeting commodity.

Realizing the critical situation, Laura grabbed the old man's hands, squeezed them, and then went to the phone. She called Doc Jones but got no response at his office. She called his home and still no response. Next, she called an ambulance agency in Lake City and described the severity of the situation. Did he have insurance or was he on welfare, a voice inquired. Presently she was told to call the county sheriff for an ambulance since it would be a costly trip for the ambulance company.

But she attempted to call Doc Jones again, and again she got no response. It sounded to her that the old man's breathing was becoming still more labored. Finally, she reached the county sheriff's dispatcher who said he would have an ambulance on the way shortly.

She tried Doc for the third time and was successful.

"Blue in the face ya say? Give 'im oxygen. He has pneumonia. I'll come up as soon as I get Mrs. McGerty's ankle taped up," the doctor advised.

She returned to the sickroom where the afternoon sun now began to stream through the window.

"Gramp, the doctor is on his way. He'll be here to help you pretty soon now."

The old man remained unresponsive. She sat down on a chair next to the bed, opened her purse, and took out a small bottle of tablets. She read the directions and then looked at Gramp. Suddenly she leaned over close to his ear and spoke softly.

"Gramp, would you like your medicine?"

She was answered by deep, irregular gasps. Now, as the late afternoon sun flooded the room, the old man's eyes became brighter. He became alert and stared westward out the window as if in anticipation. The sun's golden rays pierced the branches of a remaining oak, forming shadowy images on the windowpane. As a robin sang nearby, the image of a cross appeared on the window, and peace filled the old man's transfixed eyes.

Suddenly convulsions shook Gramp's body, followed by desperate gasping. As Laura looked on helplessly, the breathing stopped. There was a gurgle and a single exhalation. And that was all; death had come. When she glanced at Gramp's face, she noted that peace had already settled there, and the half-opened eyes still gazed out the window. She felt that at any moment he might speak and explain what he watched. But death had come, bringing relief from a long struggle, and bringing a final peace. She wondered if the ultimate peace is found only in death.

The room got brighter as the sun continued to settle. Sunlight now covered most of the bed, bathing the quiet form resting in exquisite peace. She looked out the window and observed one of the huge remaining oaks in the yard, spared because of Gramp's urgings. On one leafless bough that swooped past the window, two robins sat near an old nest wedged in among the limbs. They flew playfully around the nest, chirping and chasing. Suddenly, they perched on a small limb and began warbling. She sat listening, entranced by the sounds, now rising, now falling, sad yet beautiful.

"How is he, young lady?"

She looked up, startled, as from a dream.

"What took you so long? He's in very bad condition."

"We came right away, ma'am," the officer responded.

An attendant listening for a pulse began shaking his head negatively. "I'm sorry but there is nothing more that we can do for him." And after a short pause he asked, "Where do you want us to take him?"

Looking down at the old man with tear-laden eyes, Laura replied, "To Musselman's in Lake City."

They took Gramp away.

Gramp's Song (At Evening)

Evening and quiet,
And that old ache in my breast,
When I think of the summer rose,
And the thrush in its nest.

Then I hear the country folks a singin',
And the air is filled with glee.
For when the sun serenely sets,
I know they sing for me.

Evening and shadows,
Which close a restless day,
Oh, to hear the whippoorwills,
And smell the new-mown hay.

Then I hear the country folks a singin',
And the air is filled with glee.
For when the moon rises o'er the hill,
I know they sing for me.

Soft evening of fragrance,
Drifting with the twilight breeze,
As the lilacs and roses dance gaily,
Beneath the tall, dark trees.

I know the country folks are a singin',
Since the air is filled with glee.
Sing! And sing on through the sweet night!
Sing! And sing on for me!

XXIV.

As Ray drove the last few miles home that evening, he was in a hopeful yet feisty mood. It was only the first part of April but here was May weather. If the weather remained like this, they might begin work on the barn soon. If he could get Hibler to saw beams for just one day, he and Gramp would have enough material on hand to get a good start on the barn before spring planting. However, the incident over the money that morning still antagonized him. The audacity of the Cranes to meddle in his business. Evidently Sproule and others had something against him and were now working on Laura for some reason. He might have to let her keep the checkbook again in order to get all the money into one account. He would find ways to placate her. But he must never let Laura know about his deal with Hibler for the exchange of help. He didn't need cash from Hibler; he needed help to rebuild the barn. They had plenty of cash right now to keep going if they lived sparingly, and he would see to that. But what if Laura had decided to stay with her mother? He knew his wife well enough to know that they would not get along for very long. The mother would treat her like a child, and she would soon be back with him. She would face reality soon enough, he guessed. Besides, she liked Gramp and probably had already returned to look after him. She had nursed him through colds before, while he was in the service. As he approached the top of the hill from the west, he saw a huge moon over the hills beyond Landville. It was a beautiful evening, and he was again hopeful.

He was reassured when he turned into the driveway, for the kitchen and dining room lights were on. Gramp would not have left them on like that. He even looked forward, perhaps, to a table set for him. Laura in a conciliatory gesture might have a nice, hot meal ready.

But such was not his fortune. The kitchen was deserted, and he entered the living room where Laura quietly sat, baby in arms.

"Well, what's cookin'?" Ray approached her good-humoredly.

There was silence.

"How's Gramp?"

There was more silence. Then came a soft yet blunt expression, "He died."

Now Ray was silent and soon disbelieving. He stared down at her and the child.

"Come on. This is not a time for jokes." But the gravity of her look told the truth. He walked to the old man's bedroom and returned with a perplexed look upon his face.

"Where did they take 'im?"

"To Musselman's," came a sullen reply.

He was startled by the mention of the funeral home in Lake City. It was almost five years ago that his parents had been brought there after the tragic accident. Then it all came flooding back, the feeling of helplessness and loneliness. But all the unpleasantness had been tempered by Gramp's standing by and reassuring him.

"He died late this afternoon," Laura spoke haltingly, "and we didn't do anything to even help him." She looked down, grasping the child even tighter, as if he might be snatched away by some avenging spirit.

Then there was more silence. He glanced again at the empty bedroom and then walked to Laura and sat next to her. He looked at the little boy. Here was the end of the Lennoxes.

"I didn't know he was that sick. I thought he jist had another bad cold," Ray avowed.

"What do you think we went to town for this morning?" she answered solemnly.

He cupped his head in his hands. The turmoil of that morning seemed like ages ago. But what had occurred then faded into insignificance compared to this. It hardly seemed possible. Was Gramp really gone? Why did he die so easily? He caught bad colds every winter, and lung congestion was nothing new to him. Why did he slip away now when he was needed most? It would be more difficult now with Gramp gone. It would be different, too. But it was different when his parents went, and he managed then. Life began, life ended, and life continued. He looked at the child in its mother's arms. Here was the continuation of life. They should have more children, a more solid base to build on. They were young, and they had a whole lifetime ahead of them yet.

"The funeral home called and wanted to know about arrangements," Laura spoke, breaking into his reverie.

Arrangements again, he thought. "I'll take care of everything first thing in the morning."

The next day, Ray called both the Reverend Bruce Mattock and the funeral home. Reverend Mattock suggested that since only a few people still remembered Gramp, anyway, a brief ceremony in the funeral home would be proper. Next, Ray gave directions to the funeral home, declaring that since Gramp was not a wealthy man, he did not want one of those thousands of dollars funerals.

Two days later the brief ceremony was held in Lake City. Besides Ray and Laura, only Gramp's friends came. They included Granger, Hibler, Steinhauser, and John Crane. When the twenty minute ceremony concluded, Gramp's body was borne the twelve miles back to the Hillside Cemetery in Landville. Here overlooking the Land River, Gramp was laid to rest beside his son and daughter-in-law. It was all over by noon, and Ray and Hibler went back to work, arguing that Gramp would have wanted it that way.

That afternoon as Laura sat alone, saddened, she realized how much greater her loneliness would be now with Gramp gone. She busied herself by cleaning his room, gathering his clothes together and washing them, and collecting all his personal effects and laying them on his bed. She stared at the odd collection of relics which had been so dear to the old man. A large part of life on the hill had now gone, leaving but a few pleasant memories.

She thought about her present situation and realized that more uncertainties might develop with Gramp gone. Still she decided to stay, believing that a meaningful relationship might still develop between her and her husband. Ray had become a little more condescending, but the conflict over money had not been completely resolved.

However, as the days went by after Gramp's death, it became apparent that Ray would not change much. The funeral had cost well over two thousand dollars, a sum the funeral director had called modest. Ray complained bitterly but finally paid, taking the money from the 3,500 dollar will the old man had left them. Immediately, he put the remainder in the bank. For the sake of harmony, Laura had given in to his pleading and transferred the money from her new account to their dual account. This would make him happy, she believed. He agreed to let her have a checkbook of her own with which to do her grocery shopping. He hinted, though, that with Gramp gone less food would be required. He had even sold Gramp's old car and put the money in the bank. Life on the farm was losing its attraction for her.

For Ray, success on Oak Hill became more and more of an obsession. Outside of his property, there was little else meaningful. His family, he believed, was an integral part of the overall scheme. A successful farm would result in a successful family. Unfortunately, his failure to view the family and the property as two very different entities, each requiring a different kind of attention, resulted in an ever-widening rift between his wife and him. He worked hard for the success of his family, and he expected some appreciation for all his labors.

But it seemed as if the harder he worked, the more she complained. Now, she showed little interest in his work and plans for their future and the future of their child. Maybe if she took an active part in the work, she would be more appreciative. It was nearly May and work had not yet begun on the barn, and he was getting worried. He had enough money, but manpower was lacking. If she would learn to drive the tractor to help with the spring field work, he would be released to work on the barn.

May arrived bright and sunny. The sap was rising now and green buds were everywhere. The lilac bushes around the house had already put on deep mantels of green. A profusion of birds pecked, scratched, and chirped as they prepared their nests. High in the trees surrounding the yard, squirrels chattered, greeting the birth of a new season. Ray felt the surging fecundity all around him and was happy.

One day in early May, Hibler and two of his men came and began work on the barn. But these were old men and work was slow. Ray longed to join them and urge them on, but the field work and planting had to get done. The new barn was to be constructed with heavy pieces of timber to protect the structure against the fierce winds that periodically pounded the hill. Although Hibler had designed the barn, work went slowly because the men had difficulty setting the huge beams in place. Clearly, more manpower was required. Unless some other arrangements could be made he would have to hire some carpenters. The first crop of hay would be ready for storage in another month. The barn must be done then. He thought of Granger, but he was just another old man. Besides he was preparing for his sale and anxiously looking forward to retirement in Lake City. He decided to hire some carpenters from Lake City, but he longed to work on the barn too.

One Saturday morning as Ray was getting ready to dash out after breakfast, Laura insisted that he take the evening off so that they could go out to dinner or go to a movie in Lake City.

"I'm too busy now with all the work ta do around here," Ray answered crossly. "If you'd give me a helping hand now and then maybe we'd have more time ta go out."

"Helping hand!" she was startled. "What do you suppose I do all day in this house?"

"You don't have that much ta do always. I know ya sit around a lot. Ya could give me a hand out in the fields now when I'm so desperate," he suggested.

"A hand out in the fields!" she felt insulted.

"Don't be so funny. Plenty of farmers' wives help their husbands with field work in the spring when it's so urgent. I see 'em out driving tractor all the time. With Gramp gone, it seems like I'm twice as busy now."

"Well, I'm not going to work out in the fields. I'm not your hired man," she insisted.

"You'd be surprised how a person feels after a day's work outside. It would be good fer ya."

"No!" she emphasized.

"Well, I'll have ta hire someone then, 'n' we'll have ta tighten up even a little more," he announced.

"What are Hibler and his men doing out there?" she pointed toward the work site.

"They're takin' too long. Before we know it, there'll be crops ta put in and no place to put 'em." He got up from the table with a jerk as he spoke, rattling the dishes.

"No movie tonight then?" she asked.

"We don't have the time 'n' we can't afford it now," he snapped. "That's all I want ta hear about it."

"I'll go by myself then, and I don't want to hear any more about it," she railed.

He said nothing, went quickly into the living room, returned, and hastened out the door. She watched as he hurried to the work site where Hibler and two men were preparing for the day's work. She watched him as he pointed and talked to Hibler. He pointed at Steinhauser and the other man, waved goodbye, and then hurried up the hill where he always parked the tractor. For the first time she realized that she did not feel sorry for him while watching him. Then she heard Dylan giggle from the high chair, and she turned around and chucked him under the chin.

She decided that she would take the car that afternoon and visit her mother. She might even spend the afternoon in Lake City and top off the day with a movie. She hurried through the morning household in eager anticipation. She finished early and decided to make a list of things to shop for that day. She went into the living room to get a pen from her purse. Opening it, she discovered that both her checkbook and the car keys were gone. She was astonished and then angered. So this was all he made of promises: she could always have a checkbook, if she closed her account and transferred the money to their account.

She fumed. She had had enough of these childish tricks. He would never be fair to her. What she had thought for the past year was true: she was not really a wife, but merely property, like his machinery or oak trees. You must produce, or there is no place for you here. Go to work out in the fields! Sure, and be his little slave! He thought he was in control of everything, but she would show him. She'd leave him for a few days, and see if he took much notice of it. She'd show him!

She called her mother and explained that she would like to visit her for a couple of days. The mother insisted that she would send someone up to get her and all her belongings. Laura had to explain twice that since it was a beautiful day she preferred to walk down and that she was staying only two days. Then she got a few basic things together for the child and put them into a small handbag. She strapped Dylan into the carrier, tied him onto her back, and set out.

As she turned out of the driveway and started down Townline Road, she heard the tractor returning from the field. Then she saw a cloud of dust heading down the field toward the work site. He stopped at the work site and motioned the men toward the house. So he was inviting them in for noon dinner for a third straight day. Well, if he was so desperate to have her work in the field, evidently she was of little value in the house. Noon dinner wasn't that important, and they could get on well without her. She hurried on down behind some bushes and looked back. Soon she heard a car door slam and an engine start. She ducked into bushes along the road and continued down the hill behind them. She heard the car coming and waited behind a thick oak. The car slowly went by, stopping now and then and starting again. He was driving down the hill looking for her. She proceeded cautiously now, as the car disappeared out of sight. He obviously went to town to buy some groceries since she doubted if there was enough food on hand. Naturally, he'd be looking for her too, since he needed someone to cook the meals. She moved back onto the road again and walked briskly down the hill. As she approached the Land River Bridge about twenty minutes later, she saw him coming around the corner, just out of town. His view was marred by the bridge railing which she ducked down behind. Finally, she entered town, certain that she'd hear from him soon.

She walked through town excitedly, as if she were returning home after a long absence. People en route greeted her and asked her if she were coming back to stay. She told everyone that she was just visiting her mother for a couple of days. As she approached the Crane house, she saw her mother and Mrs. Scrang on the front lawn engaged in animated conversation. As she approached them, their conversation took on a livelier dimension.

"I seed 'im," Addie shouted to her from a block away. "Druv right down the street lookin' fer ya. We's sure he caught ya 'n' took ya back. I jist happen ta be lookin' out the winda, 'cause yer mother said you's comin', 'n' sure 'nuf he druv right down the street lookin' fer ya. I'd jist finished my nap 'n' thought I'd—"

"So," Helga broke in, "you don't have a car anymore either."

"No car and no money," came a somber reply.

Addie Scrang cocked her head a little to one side and then broke into a livid profusion of words. "I wouldn't put up with that a ta'l. Why, when Sam was alive, he always treated me like a lady. Didn't dare do anything otherwise. Always spent money on me and kept me happy. Yes, siree, only once he did somethin' nasty, 'n' he never did it again. Stayed out and played cards with the boys one night 'n' came home late in the mornin' all soused up 'n' started yellin' at me. I tell you he never done it again!" She waved a bony finger in the air while she spoke and thrust her chin determinedly forward. "No, siree, I wouldn't put up with nothin' like that. You jist—"

"Well! She's finally woke up," Helga cut in.

"Stayin' here fer good?" Addie inquired.

"No."

"You should," Addie proclaimed.

"Just for a few days, I believe," Laura concluded.

"You just stay here as long as you please. Don't go rushing back up there when he comes with one of his sad stories," the mother urged, "'n' we'll go up there tomorrow and get your belongings."

"Let's wait a few days," Laura insisted.

XXV.

When Ray found the house empty at noon, he concluded that Laura had gone for a walk, purposely to spite him and the men. How silly she was. The little things she'd try to do to get even. But a walk in the country might do her some good. She did not respect plants and animals enough. If she got outside more often, she might learn to appreciate farm life. She always pretended that she was living in town, here on the farm. He wondered if she'd ever adapt to farming. Anyway he'd have to drive downtown to the store to get some food for the men. If he saw her, he wouldn't even stop for her. Let her walk a little bit. It would do her some good.

He got back to the house after dark that day, planned to eat a hot supper and then return to the field. He was surprised to find the house dark and empty. So she did defy him and sneak out to see a movie. Her relatives must be somehow involved. They were always butting in and trying to bait her away whenever a little problem developed. It made him angry to think that she had time to enjoy herself while he had to work and slave away for their living.

Several days went by, and he didn't hear from her. He did not get concerned. He would play her little game and see how long she could stand her mother. She left everything: clothes, jewelry, makeup. It was obvious that she planned to come back soon. He would let a week elapse and then call his mother-in-law.

Laura soon discovered that her newly-found freedom was actually enjoyable. Surprisingly, she did not miss life on the farm. However, she often thought about Ray and wondered how he could do both farm work and house work.

The Cranes supported her both emotionally and materially. She began wearing old clothes from her high school days and felt younger again. The villagers were also very supportive and praised her for her wise decision. Whenever she remonstrated and suggested that it was time to return to the hill, they argued that she should wait a little longer, just to make sure. On the fifth day of her exile, she decided that it was time for her and Dylan to return to the hill to see how things were going. However, some of the villagers, supported by her mother, pointed out that Ray hadn't shown the slightest concern since she had left him. He had been to town and not even mentioned her name. Some even suggested that he might be seeing Judy Hamilton, an old friend who now was a secretary in Lake City. Laura listened with interest to all the suggestions and counsel. She wondered why she should return to an inattentive husband. Thus a week went by, and one evening Ray called.

"So, when are ya comin' back?" he began.

There was a pause.

"Oh, in another week, I guess. I've been so busy here. There's something going on all the time here," she declared.

"Well, all the hard work's over now, 'n' you wouldn't have ta do much. The barn is well on its way up, too. You'd be surprised at how much better the place looks already. I think you'd really enjoy the summer up here. Oh, I almost forgot. I planted a little garden. Nothin' like Gramp's of course. But there'll be plenty of fresh lettuce, radishes, and carrots pretty soon. Remember how you 'n' Gramp used ta enjoy goin' out in the garden ta get fresh vegetables ta take home ta Landville?"

"Oh, yes, that all seems so long ago now," she responded casually.

There was another pause.

"Well, I miss you 'n' was hopin' you'd come back pretty soon," he got to the point.

"Oh, I guess I'll be back in another week or so," she replied nonchalantly.

"Good, I'll come down 'n' git you and Dylan in another week then. I haven't seen him fer so long. How is he doin'?"

"Oh, he's really growing now and starting ta get into things. Mom has to keep everything out of reach. He's turning into quite a little guy."

"I'll see both of ya next week then, O.K.?"

"O.K." she echoed.

"Good-bye."

"Bye, bye."

There was more silence and she slowly hung up.

June arrived and the second week came. But then, an event occurred which affected her outlook and her thoughts of where she belonged. One evening Everett Ernst called and invited her to dinner and to a concert over in Lake City. Immediately, she became excited with thoughts of a glamorous night out in the big city. At first, she was uncertain of how to respond to the invitation. But, she thought, it's only a casual get-together for old times' sake. There was no harm in that, and a date was made for Saturday evening, only two days before Ray was scheduled to come and get her. She would have at least one big evening out before returning to the boring routine of the farm. Although it would be just a harmless escapade, she felt a little uneasy.

"Foolishness! He'll never know the difference," her mother interposed. "Besides, you don't know what all he's been doin' up there all by himself. That Hamilton girl was always after him, and she's still around. Don't worry about it. It's all fair and square now."

All week she thought about the coming Saturday evening. She worried about formalities and the impression she'd make on the newspaper man. After all, she had not been out on a formal date since junior prom in high school. She felt better after her mother bought her a stylish new dress, including new shoes. When she dressed up and modeled before the mirror, she felt like a new person, hardly like a farmer's wife. In fact she felt important to someone, someone special. As Saturday drew near, she became more excited. Whenever she voiced her fears and doubts about the rightness of the date, she was criticized by both friends and family: she was doing the proper thing; there was nothing to worry about; this was her one big chance; she should get out and enjoy herself. She began to think that there was no harm in going out to dinner with an old friend. In the flush of the excitement, she scarcely thought about Oak Hill and the husband who eagerly awaited her arrival home.

The big evening finally came, and she set out for a spectacular time with Ev, as he was affectionately called. They ate at what he called a "premier" restaurant and saw a "quality" show. With the dinner, theater, and dancing late into the night, she had a beautiful time which ended too quickly. She eagerly accepted his offer to escort her to a dinner-dance the next Saturday evening.

Sunday evening arrived, and Laura grew worried since she wasn't set on returning to Oak Hill.

"I just don't feel ready to go back up there yet," she admitted. "I'd like to go to that big dance next Saturday night."

"Well, there's no sense in goin' back if you believe there's something more important for you. It's about time you got something out of life, instead of wasting away," the mother counseled.

"But he's coming tomorrow and figures I'll want to go back with him," she lamented.

"If you don't feel like doing something, then ya shouldn't do it. He'll jist go on in the same old ways and you'll be jist as unhappy as ever. Call him and tell him you're not feeling well. There's a little flu goin' around now. Tell him you've caught it. Call him first thing in the morning, or you stay in bed and I'll call him."

"No, I'll do it."

So, Laura called Ray early the next morning and explained her illness.

"Flu's going around town now. I just felt dizzy this morning and thought I'd better let you know at least. I plan to see Doc if I don't get better by tomorrow."

Ray listened sympathetically and realized that he couldn't afford to get sick now at the height of the working season. He decided it would be best to wait.

"Oh, I'm sorry ta hear it. I'm sure you'll feel better soon." There was a pause. Each waited for the other to say something. "I'll call you back on Wednesday 'n' plan to git ya on Thursday," Ray finally continued.

"Well, how about waiting 'til next Sunday instead? There's so much Mother and I wanted to do this week, and now I'll be laid up for awhile. Next Sunday would be much better."

"I miss ya, hon, 'n' Sunday's so far away. Besides I'm so anxious to see little Dylan again. It's been so long. I might still drive down one night this week."

"We'll be gone visiting some evenings later during the week, so it might be hard to plan for something like that," Laura admonished.

Laura languished in the house for a few days, and the news quickly spread around the village that she was ill. Ernst heard the news, and on Wednesday, Laura received a bouquet of red roses with a note attached, "I hope this brings you a little cheer, Ev." Laura was astonished and charmed by the flowers, for she had never received a bouquet in her life. Ray had given her several corsages for school dances, but never so many beautiful flowers as these. The roses were placed in a vase and set on the kitchen table where they were admired by mother and daughter.

Laura, lost in thoughts about Ev, was quiet most of the week. She dreamed of him, admired him, and longed for him. Would Saturday night ever come? A strange mixture of melancholy and joy pervaded her: she wanted Ev, yet there was Ray.

Ray in his anxiety worked harder than ever, from dawn to dusk, thinking frequently of Laura and Dylan. Why had she left him so suddenly? They had always resolved their disagreements, and the one over the money wasn't that serious. It, too, could quickly be resolved because she was a sensible girl. She loved the house he had given her. She most certainly would be anxious to get back by now.

He decided that Sunday would definitely be the end of the estrangement. He would go down and get his wife and child and that would be the end of it. If it weren't the busy season, he'd have stopped the nonsense long ago. But after spending so much time away, maybe she'd appreciate the farm more now.

He decided to be polite yet firm with both mother and daughter. Most women, he believed, were alike. Make a promise, followed by a little affection, and you have them. He knew that he had been neglecting Laura, but she was an understanding girl. He also knew what was best for the Lennox family, and they'd all be back together on the hill soon.

He had worked hard for his family the past two years. They had overcome all the setbacks, and everything was nearly back to normal again. The barn was well on its way up, the crops were flourishing, and the weather had remained quite favorable. To get Laura back again would top off the success of the spring. Although there was no source of income yet, he would explain his plans for the summer to her: the selling of more oak and the purchasing of cattle. They would have a lot of money coming in soon.

She had got sick. That's what happened when a person left the country and went to town. Gramp had told him many times that country people were stronger and healthier than city folks. If she'd stayed up on the hill, she probably wouldn't be suffering now. Down there in the village there was always disease and hardship. In the large cities, there was uncontrollable crime and the worst of lawlessness. In the country at least people were a little more sane and didn't prey on one another. Yes, he would soon go down into the dark valley and bring her back to the light of the hill. Her relatives were probably behind it all anyway, putting foolish notions in her head and polluting her outlook on life. And then there was his son. The boy must be returned to the hill because he was at an impressionable age now and liable to silly notions. Soon he'd be completely spoiled for life. Yes, Sunday would be a crucial day, and he was certain everything would turn out favorably.

XXVI.

SUNDAY MORNING DAWNED, AND Laura was still not at home. She had gone to the gala dinner and ball and was in a state of elation all evening. Never had she met so many famous people, people who were wealthy, popular, and fun to be with. Many mistook her for Ev's wife, a mistake she gloried in. Afterwards, they had gone to Ev's plush apartment, where the newspaper man had mixed them drinks, something she had rarely had before. They talked for awhile, and then Ernst, who had been drinking most of the evening, made love to her. She submitted easily as if it were the natural thing to do with Ev. Finally, when he took her home at 10:30 in the morning, she was euphoric. Never had she felt that way with Ray. However, she was puzzled that Ev didn't invite her out the following weekend.

When Ray arrived at the Crane house at one o'clock Sunday afternoon, Laura was still in bed.

"She's been sick most of the week," the mother fabricated.

"She needs a little fresh country air, that's all. The sooner she gits home, the better off she'll be. She's homesick," Ray testified.

"Homesick when she's already home!" Helga argued.

Ray did not respond but looked at Dylan who was sitting on the sofa staring and waving at him. When Ray picked up the child, he began to cry.

"I guess he just doesn't know who you are," Helga hastened to comment with a giggle.

"Hush that now, little Dylan. Daddy's come ta take you and Mommy back home. Ya want to go back, don't ya?" The little boy stopped crying and pushed away from his father's face.

"He's had a great time here, all the toys and things he wants. He'll hate to leave," the grandmother speculated.

"Well, I kin see he's a little spoiled already, 'n' soon I won't be able to do a thing with 'im," Ray complained.

"He's not spoiled, that's for certain. He's been learning the proper ways of behavior here."

Ray became irritated. "I know what the proper ways are 'n' that's what we'll all be goin' back ta pretty soon," he declared.

"I think Laura's starting to look at it different though," the mother-in-law hinted.

"You jist let me talk ta her about that. I'll go upstairs 'n' talk to her now."

"She's awfully sick. Had a rough night last night. Even missed church this morning. Why don't you come back in a week or so when she's feeling better?"

"You think she's that sick? She's not sick. She's jist gotten lazy, and the more she lays around down here the sicker she'll git. This whole thing's gone on long enough. I'll give 'er another hour. I'm takin' a walk around town and'll be back. She'd better be up then," he threatened.

"We'll see," Helga Crane replied.

As Ray headed along the few blocks leading downtown, he came to the road leading up to the cemetery, and he decided to take it. He had plenty of time for a little stroll to the top of the hill. Besides, the view overlooking the village and river was spectacular. As he looked up the hill, he saw the usual white clouds drifting along. They always seemed to be attracted by the huge oaks up there. The trees themselves were monuments, not allowed to be cut since the woods belonged to the village. It was a quiet, peaceful Sunday as he began the climb. The countryside was full of an assortment of chirpings and tweetings. Meadowlarks, perched on fence posts along the way, sang jovially back and forth to one another. Some even hopped from post to post, following him as he walked. Squirrels, disturbed by an intruder in their sanctuary, chattered high in the trees as he passed. Frequently, rabbits hopped into the weeds along the road. It was a beautiful day in June, and he breathed deeply of the fresh air.

Halfway up the hill, on a gently rolling plateau, he came to the entrance of the Landville Hillside Cemetery. He paused for a moment, looked further up the hill, and then walked in among the tombstones. He glanced at names on the stone monuments as he strode along to the Lennox plot. The names were familiar. From his boyhood, he remembered the people behind the names. It all seemed so long ago—the old gray ones who limped along Main Street with their canes and sat gossiping on the benches there. He remembered. He stopped at the Crane plot and looked at the tombstones of Laura's father and paternal grandparents. He remembered Laura's father, a man who always treated his family well. Laura was like her father, kind and sympathetic. But now she seemed to be under the sway of her mother, and he wondered. Well, he would soon have a good talk with her, and they would settle the matter. He noted that on the father's tombstone, a space had been reserved for Mrs. Crane, with her first name and birth date already engraved.

He arrived at the Lennox plot and noted that Gramp did not have a tombstone. There was just a small marker imbedded in the ground with his name and dates on it. The grave still looked fresh with newly-lain sod over it. As he quietly stood beside the graves, a vague longing filled his being. He yearned for the past and the loved ones who rested beneath the soil, but he also dreamed of the future and the building of a new family of Lennoxes. How uncertain life was, and he wondered at times if he was building in vain. He wondered if his dreams would ever be realized. He could not imagine living without a family to build for. But his wife and child were coming home soon. There was hope. Then he glanced at the gravestone of his mother and father. They had worked so hard and had accomplished so little. Whenever he thought of them at rest up here, he questioned the meaning of existence. Was life no more than the continuation of one death followed by another? Was living no more than the perpetual picking up of the pieces? He did not like these thoughts. He would go and get Laura now and they would go home.

As he started out, he glanced toward the western hills where, prominently growing out of one of them, was the new barn, a bold and rugged structure. It symbolized the Lennoxes, he thought, and would last as long as the hills. No fierce winds would ever take it down.

Ray glanced into the valley below as he headed down. The Land River glistened under the bright afternoon sun. From nearly all the bridges upstream, he saw fishermen busy taking their afternoon catch. Downstream, beyond the sawmill, he saw no one. The village was resting peacefully on the Sabbath. There were few people in the streets and little traffic. Off the road to his right, he spotted a bright patch of wild violets. He picked a large bouquet for Laura and hurried on. She loved flowers and had always taken good care of the lilacs and roses on the hill. She missed all the beautiful lilacs this year, he thought.

It wasn't quite 2:00 yet, and he decided to take a quick stroll downtown. The downtown was deserted save for a few elderly men who were sitting on a bench in front of the Oakwood Tavern. They were in animated laughter. However, when they saw him, they became strangely quiet.

"Hi fellas!" Ray greeted.

They all acknowledged the greeting and stared at him.

"Nice day," Ray indicated.

"Yep, couldn't be nicer," Joe Yankel replied.

"Where ya goin' to with all them flowers?" a well-dressed elderly gentleman asked.

"Oh, I picked 'em for my wife. She loves flowers," Ray explained.

"They're pretty. Will she be goin' home to the hill soon?" Ben Rawler asked.

"Yep, today, as soon as I get over there," Ray answered.

The three men looked at each other furtively and then, finally, fixed a stare upon Ray as he began to leave.

"We heerd she got a boyfriend now," Ben blurted out. "But I ain't gonna say nothin' about it."

Ray was silent as the statement shot through him like poison.

"What do ya mean, a boyfriend?" The violets began to burn in his hand.

"I ain't sayin' nothin'," Ben reminded.

"It's that big smarty-pants, Ernst," Joe Yankel spoke, deciding to scoop everyone.

"That's right," the well-dressed gent agreed.

Ray stared at them angrily, at a loss for words. Then he glanced at the flowers in his hand and walked quickly toward the Crane house. He squeezed the violets tightly in his fist and then let them drop to the pavement. So Ernst was behind it all. He should have realized there was something the matter after she stayed away so long. Maybe he ought to go to his fancy apartment and take care of him first. But he decided to get it straight from her first and then act.

He pounded on the Crane door and then quickly walked through the unlocked entrance. He immediately confronted Laura who was sitting and drinking coffee with her mother at the kitchen table.

"What were you doin' last night?" he growled.

"She was home sick in bed all night," the mother defended.

Laura, after looking at the anger in her husband's eyes, spoke softly to him, "Ray let's go for a little walk and get this all settled." She gently touched his hand as she spoke.

"It's best be settled right here," the mother recommended.

Ray looked angrily at his wife and then muttered, "O.K., let's go."

Laura led the way to the door. They walked slowly down the sidewalk as both Helga Crane and Addie Scrang watched through their living room windows.

"Ray, there's something I've got ta tell you, and it's so hard to do. But please don't be angry because it's all out of our control now."

They continued in silence down the street. "I know I was wrong in doing it, but I've been seeing Ev Ernst."

"A guy with a reputation like his?" Ray declared.

Laura ignored the statement and went on, "I was getting so lonely up there with nothing of interest for me. And you always trying to tie me down with farm work."

"But still I've been good to ya. I've given ya a home. I know I neglected you a little 'n' left ya alone sometimes, but I couldn't leave the work undone. I'm doin' it all for you," Ray pleaded.

"I know you always meant well, but I realize now that I'm not suited for life on a farm. I've found an entirely different world down here which I never realized existed until I left it for awhile."

"But we kin make a go of it this time. This time it won't be so bad for ya. I've got everything in good shape up there now, and it's all waiting fer you to come back."

"Oh Ray," she began sobbing, "I hate to say this. It was a mistake for me to move up there with you. I thought I loved you and would love you forever," she spoke through sobs, "but that's changed now. If you only knew how free I've felt the past two weeks. I just can't go up there anymore."

They stopped beneath a huge oak.

"Jist one more try, hon. It'll all be different this time, I promise." He took her hands and caressed them. "You can have whatever ya want ta fix the house up."

"If you only knew how many times I've given it one more try during the last year. Many times I'd decided to leave but then changed my mind for one more try. Each time, I was always sorry. I'm happy here, Ray."

He was silent.

"But why Ernst? You must know what he is. He's got women all over."

"That's the gossip we always heard. He says he loves me. I just can't waste anymore of my life." She was sobbing again.

"There's no point in me askin' ya back then?"

"Please, Ray, I've told you how I feel. I belong down here. There's no life, no future for me up there."

"And that's why you deserted me, for Ernst?"

"Don't make it so hard, Ray." She spoke through tears, "I love Ev and that's all that matters now."

"You'll be sorry some day. Jist wait 'n' see," he murmured.

"Why don't we both just be free for a few months. It might blow over. I'm so confused now. Please, Ray?" She grabbed his arms and gazed steadily into his eyes. "Please, let's not become enemies. You can go out with other girls, too. That's fair enough, isn't it?"

He was lost in thought.

"Who'll support ya?" he wondered.

"I've managed O.K. the past few weeks. My relatives are taking good care of us. I've even thought of looking for a job over in Lake City."

"What can ya do?"

"I'm a good typist. I'll brush up on my typing. They're always looking for secretaries in the state offices. I might even go back to school."

There was another pause.

"Well, I don't know what ta say anymore. I s'pose I have no choice now," he concluded. "Ya don't want a divorce? Ya might want ta return to me some day, is that it?"

"I just don't care for that kind of life. Those long days when I hardly see you. Maybe you could get a job in town, too. That's what you should have done in the first place. You had all those nice offers from my uncle," she persisted.

"No, my place will be up there with or without you. I giss there's no point in discussing this any further. We might as well let this thing ride for awhile. Besides, like ya said, there are other girls. But I expect ta see Dylan sometime." They started back toward the house.

"Oh, that's no problem. Come down anytime during the week or whenever. We could even come up to see you now and then, if you want."

He said nothing.

They approached his car. "I'm sorry it didn't work out, Ray, but did you ever really love me?"

He opened the door and, as he got into the car, responded, "Yes, I loved you." He started the car, eyes now moist, and drove away. She watched until the car disappeared around a corner.

XVII.

A WEEK AND A HALF passed and there was no sign of Ernst. She and her mother began to worry. Had he been offended? Was he out of town on some story? When Helga Crane called the newspaper's main office in Lake City, she was told that Ernst had gone out of state for awhile. The man would not tell her exactly why.

"Funny he didn't say anything ta you," Helga protested.

"He said he'd see me soon," Laura assured.

"Next time we see him in church, we'll invite him over for stuffed pork chops and find out what's going on," the mother declared.

But Ernst didn't show up in church.

Laura really missed Ev and wondered if he was avoiding her for some reason. She had done nothing to insult him. It must have been some urgent business that drew him away. If she could get an address she would write to him and express her feelings about him. Anyway, she knew that he would call soon. They had had such a marvelous time together. Certainly he missed her as much as she missed him.

One morning Ray called and said that he planned to drop down the next evening for a short visit. Everything was blooming and booming on the hill, he bragged. He hoped the rain would hold off for a few more days so that they could finish the roofing on the barn. They had hay in now and couldn't afford to get it wet. Laura invited him down and even hinted that she would be glad to see him again.

The next morning was gray and threatening. As Laura looked out from her upstairs bedroom, she could see dark clouds gathering in the west. A gathering whirlwind, Gramp always called such storms. They always seemed to swirl in over the western hills in a fury. But the village, sheltered down in the valley, always escaped the worst of it. The clouds look so dark today, she thought. Well, she would just have to stay in. Besides, Ray wouldn't be able to do much and probably would be down early. She hadn't missed the farm at all, but it would be nice to see him again. Then rain began to patter against the windows, and thunder rolled through the skies. A severe storm was brewing. But farmers always liked plenty of rain this time of year, and Ray would be no exception.

She sat down at a table that was still set for her, and her mother joined her for more coffee. Dylan, who had already been fed, was back in his crib in the living room.

Laura was about to start her second cup of coffee when they heard a siren. It seemed to be going north toward Lake City, now in a terrible downpour.

"I suppose someone got struck by lightning," Helga suggested.

"I hope not," Laura responded. "These storms are always so nasty this time of year."

After breakfast, Laura went to the bathroom mirror to prepare herself. Because of the bad storm, Ray probably would pay her a visit since he could do no outside work. She stared at herself in the mirror and thought how nice it would be to look beautiful like a movie star and be sought after by many. What shade of lipstick should she use and how much makeup, if any? She began to prepare her hair in the style that always pleased Ray.

Suddenly the wind began to howl and intense rain lashed against the house. As it became darker, her features became darkly represented in the mirror. She was still combing her hair when there was a knock at the front door. Her heart jumped! Was it Ray? Had he driven through the awful storm to visit her? She raced to the door, arriving before her mother. Opening the door, she saw a policeman.

"Mrs. Lennox?"

"Yes?" Her voice was full of wonder.

"I'm sorry to report that your husband was badly injured this morning and was taken to the hospital in Lake City."

"Injured? How?"

"We don't know for sure. Other workmen were there. He was calling for you. I can take you over if you'd like."

"How bad was he hurt?" Helga inquired.

"He's not good," the officer replied, "but we all know the facilities are great in Lake City."

"I've got to go! Take care of Dylan!" Laura urged her mother.

"How long ago did it happen?" Helga inquired.

"It's been nearly an hour now, but they got 'im to the hospital in a hurry," the officer replied.

As Laura grabbed her purse, raincoat, and umbrella, she wondered if this was a bad dream. Could Ray actually be injured and in the hospital—the one who was so young and strong, the one who was always in control, the one who would stop for nothing? But he was calling for her now, and she must respond. This was reality. She felt glum as they drove through the darkness and the pouring rain.

They entered the hospital and met Hibler and Steinhauser who were at the front desk speaking to a nurse.

"What happened to Ray?" she implored. "How is he?"

"O.K., I giss," Hibler intoned.

Soon a doctor approached.

"Mrs. Lennox? Please sit." The doctor pointed to a chair. "Your husband arrived by ambulance over an hour ago with severe head and neck injuries. He needed immediate neuro-surgery. We were preparing him for surgery in the trauma center; unfortunately, his cranial injuries were fatal." His voice dropped. "I'm sorry, but your husband expired before we could initiate the surgery."

She said nothing, but looked down and cupped her forehead in her hands.

"He's died then, did you say?"

"His injuries were such that there was little we could do here except release some of the pressure. We did everything possible under the circumstances," the doctor replied.

She remained silent and then looked at him, tears in her eyes. "I would like to see Ray now."

"Surely." The doctor helped her up. "Can you make it alone?"

"Yes."

They walked down a long corridor and stopped in front of a door. The doctor asked her to remain outside for a moment, and he went in. Shortly, he opened the door and invited her in.

Ray lay on a cot, his arms lying straight along each side. A white sheet, rolled back, covered the bottom part of his body. His hands looked so strange, she thought, so motionless. These were the hands that worked so hard, the hands that held her hands so many times. He wore his favorite blue-plaid shirt, the one he wore the last time she saw him. She gazed steadily at the pale face and wished the eyes would open to life for just one moment. His brown hair, snarled and damp-looking, was swept back over one ear. She noted marks on his forehead. He looked so peaceful now, no more struggles or worries.

Then she thought about her past life with Ray: the strong, fleet halfback, admired by the villagers; the handsome, young soldier, respected by all; and the energetic, honest farmer, her husband, and the man she would always love. She took his hand in hers and began to weep openly. Soon, she felt an arm around her shoulder.

"Mrs. Lennox, we'd better go now," and the doctor gently guided her away.

"We're sorry about all this," Hibler muttered.

"Ja, ver sorry," Steinhauser repeated.

She remained silent and stared out a window to the south where a rainbow was forming.

Hibler continued, "We told 'im ta stay off that roof 'cause of the storm, but ya know Ray."

"What did he want up on the roof during a storm?" Laura asked, her face in surprise.

"Well, ya know, there was a little corner to be shingled yet. Woulda taken a couple of us no more than five minutes. He was so afraid rain would get into the hay, so he had ta climb up 'n' do the work. 'Twas already sprinkling when he went up."

"He fell clear off the top!" Laura responded.

"No," Hibler continued. "He finished the top 'n' was comin' back down. A big gust of wind hit the ladder jist as he was gettin' on it. It twisted away from 'im and he fell. It was rainin' hard by then and awful slippery. He jist couldn't git a hold anywhere 'n' fell."

"Ja, ve try to helf, aber could do notting," Steinhauser added.

"We were down loadin' the truck, 'n' we heard 'im yell. If we was a little closer, we mighta catched 'im," Hibler allowed.

After a short silence, Hibler suggested that they leave for Landville.

"Mrs. Lennox?" A nurse spoke as they were getting ready to leave. "May I speak to you for a moment?"

"Yes."

"Where do you want us to take Ray?" Laura paused, confused.

"What mortuary, ma'am?"

After a short pause, she answered softly, "Musselman's."

The day of Ray's funeral was bright and sunny. The ceremony was attended by many people. Laura, who had been brooding since the death, began to feel better after hearing all the ringing praises. Many people gathered around her, clasped her hand, and offered their sympathies. During the service, all the Cranes sat in the front pews. Mrs. Crane even invited Mrs. Addie Scrang to join them there. After a short biography and a hymn, the Reverend Bruce Mattock delivered a short eulogy in which he praised the gifts and service of fine young men like Ray. Then Ray was borne away to the Hillside Cemetery and laid to rest beside his grandfather.

To Laura, it seemed odd to be standing on the same spot where two months ago Gramp had been buried. Now the young man had joined the old one. She glanced west and observed the new red barn through the trees. How strange death is, she thought—the tragic death which claimed him, on the land he loved, and on the building which obsessed him. How strange—across the valley from the hillside of work and toil to the hillside of peace and rest. Ray loved the hills, and she would see that he got a proper monument.

After the internment, close friends and relatives returned to the church parlor for lunch. The praises continued. Addie Scrang voiced a strong approval of the young man. "He was a fine fella. I remember once when I had a flat jist this side o' the bridge. He comes along, 'n' I know he was in a hurry, too. Had the old truck. He comes along 'n' changed that flat in no time. There was no finer fella nowheres. He always—"

"He was a hard worker," John cut in, "and I always admired him for that. We would have made good business partners. I'll miss him."

"And gone at such a young age," Helga interjected.

"He had such a lovely farm. I s'pose it's all yours now," Mrs. Scrang, her head cocked askew, looked diligently into Laura's eyes.

"Oh, I don't know," Laura responded, irritated by the snoopiness.

"Well, you'd better git it," Helga Crane answered boldly.

Then the Reverend Bruce Mattock, with a piece of chocolate cake in hand, came over to speak to her. "May I offer once again my deepest condolence. We all loved

Ray and will miss him. If I may be of further assistance in any way, please don't hesitate to call upon me."

Hibler and Steinhauser, leaving the church, spoke briefly to her.

"We're goin' now ta do some odds 'n' ends Ray needed to finish. We'll also see that the fields get taken care of, if you'd like."

"Thanks, Fred. That would be a big help," she answered.

That evening, Laura, her mother, and Uncle John went to the farm at Helga's urging.

"After all," the mother insisted, "we'll need money to pay for the funeral."

They went directly to the living room writing desk where Ray kept his papers. In one drawer they found vaccination forms and discharge papers from the army, several watches, a little cash, and, in its original box, his gold wedding ring. Laura picked it up, studied it, and carefully placed it in her purse. In another drawer, they found among other things the checkbook, some old photographs and, in a large brown envelope, the will.

Laura owned everything: the buildings, the land, and all cash accounts. She was astonished because now she even owned Gramp's house in Landville. Two houses, land, trees, crops, and machinery, and even the barn, were hers now. It was hard to believe that everything was hers so suddenly. But she would take good care of his things. She knew how he loved the farm, and she would carry on in a way that would please him.

"I might move back for the summer," she said as they continued their search. "He has that beautiful garden that someone will have to take care of."

"You can come up from town ta do that," her mother replied.

On top of the writing desk, under a recent newspaper, they found Laura's engagement picture. In the lower right-hand corner, Laura had written, "Love forever." She had written that pledge so long ago, she thought. It seemed like a different world now.

She carefully placed the picture in her purse.

"Well, I guess we'd better go. It's gotten dark already," John advised. "We've got all the important stuff."

"Sure, we'll come back tomorrow and straighten things out. Just look at the mess he left in the kitchen," Helga complained.

Laura said nothing as they started for the car.

"You ought to sellout and invest in commercial property somewhere. There's a lot of money in that now," John recommended.

"'n' fix up the old man's house in town 'n' sell it. You kin always move in with me," her mother suggested.

"You probably should have an auction right away, too. You'd be surprised how much money they bring in," John pointed out.

"There'll be some nice cash from those crops this fall too," Helga averred, "and now you'll finally get your chance to go to the university in Lake City."

"You've got a brand new life now with plenty of security," John added.

Their voices droned on as the car headed down the hill in the dark, east, toward Landville.